P9-DZA-609

"You should move back," he told her, his voice rough sounding.

"I should," she agreed, sounding bemused and dazed. "I want to, I know I must, but I can't."

He released a groan and inhaled a solid hit of her scent. Instead of pulling away, his thumb slid over her knuckles. Passion flared in her eyes, her breath hitched and she tipped her head back, lifting her mouth. What else could he do but lower his mouth to hers?

He was an inch from her mouth, and anticipation hummed through his veins when she slapped her hand on her chest and pulled back.

"We shouldn't. I work for you," Lex told him, the expression on her face yearning. She wanted his mouth on hers as much as he wanted his there.

"Tell me not to kiss you, Cole," Lex begged.

"I can't," he whispered, bending his knees a little to meet her mouth.

He was about to make contact when voices coming from the passage pulled him back to the present. Cole stepped away from Lex and a cold dose of reality slapped him in the face.

Cape Town Tycoons

How do you resist an irresistible billionaire?

Lex and Addi Satchell had only ever had each other to rely on...until their absentee mother dropped two young sisters they never knew about on their doorstep. Now, everything Lex and Addi do is for them. They don't have time for love or passion—or to think about either!

Then Cole Thorpe and Jude Fisher come into their lives... The two tycoons are devastatingly handsome and infuriatingly tempting. So much so that working with them forces Lex and Addi to realize they aren't impervious to the attraction that Cole and Jude make them feel!

Read Cole and Lex's story in
The Nights She Spent with the CEO

And discover Jude and Addi's story,
The Baby Behind Their Marriage Merger

Coming soon!

Joss Wood

———

THE NIGHTS SHE SPENT WITH THE CEO

HARLEQUIN

PRESENTS

If you purchased this book without a cover you should be aware
that this book is stolen property. It was reported as "unsold and
destroyed" to the publisher, and neither the author nor the
publisher has received any payment for this "stripped book."

Recycling programs
for this product may
not exist in your area.

ISBN-13: 978-1-335-73917-9

The Nights She Spent with the CEO

Copyright © 2023 by Joss Wood

All rights reserved. No part of this book may be used or reproduced in
any manner whatsoever without written permission except in the case of
brief quotations embodied in critical articles and reviews.

This is a work of fiction. Names, characters, places and incidents
are either the product of the author's imagination or are used fictitiously.
Any resemblance to actual persons, living or dead, businesses,
companies, events or locales is entirely coincidental.

For questions and comments about the quality of this book,
please contact us at CustomerService@Harlequin.com.

Harlequin Enterprises ULC
22 Adelaide St. West, 41st Floor
Toronto, Ontario M5H 4E3, Canada
www.Harlequin.com

Printed in U.S.A.

Joss Wood loves books and traveling—especially to the wild places of southern Africa and, well, anywhere. She's a wife, a mom to two teenagers and a slave to two cats. After a career in local economic development, she now writes full-time. Joss is a member of Romance Writers of America and Romance Writers of South Africa.

Books by Joss Wood

Harlequin Presents

The Rules of Their Red-Hot Reunion

Scandals of the Le Roux Wedding

The Billionaire's One-Night Baby
The Powerful Boss She Craves
The Twin Secret She Must Reveal

South Africa's Scandalous Billionaires

How to Undo the Proud Billionaire
How to Win the Wild Billionaire
How to Tempt the Off-Limits Billionaire

Harlequin Desire

Wrong Brother, Right Kiss
Lost and Found Heir
The Secret Heir Returns
Crossing Two Little Lines

Visit the Author Profile page
at Harlequin.com for more titles.

CHAPTER ONE

Lᴇx sᴛᴏᴏᴅ ɪɴ the arrivals hall at Cape Town International airport, an iced coffee in one hand and a battered Thorpe Industries sign in the other. She kept meaning to make another one but, between her part-time jobs, ferrying her sisters to their after-school activities, supervising homework, making dinner and studying towards her degree, time was short.

The little things tended to fall between the cracks—such as signs.

Lex blew a copper curl out of her eyes and, when it refused to budge, she used her baby finger to pull it back and tuck it behind her ear. She'd pulled her too-long hair into a loose braid but it was already falling apart. She needed a hair cut, a facial, a massage, two million dollars…

Lex looked at the electronic board and then at her phone, checking the time. The incoming flight from London had landed fifteen minutes ago, so she could expect the passengers to start walking through any moment now.

She'd picked up many Thorpe Industries employees over the past couple of years and wondered who she'd get this time. Sometimes she'd get a talker, wide-eyed and excited about being in Africa, and she'd be peppered with questions, which she answered as best she could. Sometimes she got someone glued to their phone, who either spent the trip back to their hotel or to Thorpe Industries' headquarters looking at their tablet or taking and making calls and answering emails.

She frequently had to resist the urge to interrupt their scrolling or incessant work-based conversation to tell them to look out of the window, to take in the world-famous Table Mountain—sometimes covered by its cloud table cloth, sometimes not.

She wanted to point out the endless sea curling around the land, wild in winter, calm in summer. She wanted to remind them that they were in one of the most beautiful cities in the world, to take the moment, to haul in a breath, to pick up their heads and look at something besides their screens. But she kept her mouth shut and drove, because that was her job, and it was one she needed.

Flexible, well-paying jobs were not easy to come by.

Lex sipped her coffee, hoping that the extra hit of caffeine from the double espresso would soon kick in. Last night she'd fallen asleep at the dining room table, somewhere around two. Studying for her degree in Forensic Psychology was something she only got to after Nixi and Snow went to sleep and, invariably, when she was exhausted. She was passing her modules, but she wished she had the time to do better, to dive deeper into the subject. She didn't like being average, or not living up to her potential, but there was only a finite number of hours in the day.

You're doing the best you can. It's all anyone can ask of you. It's all you can ask of yourself.

But it still felt as if she were walking a tight rope above a sky-high canyon, about to plunge onto the jagged rocks below. Right now, the rope was tight and steady, and she knew where to put her feet. If the wind picked up or someone else jumped on the rope, she'd lose her balance and do a rope-free bungee jump.

Life had to keep ticking along just as it was, with no interruptions or distractions.

Lex noticed that the passengers from the London flight were starting to trickle into the arrival hall. Lifting her sign, she sipped her coffee, wondering whether the tall blonde wearing white linen trousers would be her pick-up, or the geeky-looking guy wearing horn-rimmed glasses. No, these were the first-class passengers and, while she'd had one or two pick-ups who were that far up the corporate ladder, most of her pick-ups either flew business class or economy.

The airport was busy and there was always something, or someone, to capture her attention. Two little boys of no more than four or five, were bouncing up and down, thoroughly over-excited at the thought of seeing Daddy, Mummy or Grandma. A thin woman stood opposite her, her arms tightly folded, staring at the ground, looking as if she'd rather be anywhere but here, meeting the person coming off that plane. There was a lull in passengers coming through the tunnel and Lex shifted from foot to foot, turning her head to look behind her.

Taller than most, at six two or six three, and dressed in solid black, he immediately caught her attention. Lex cocked her head, enjoying the view of his broad shoulders and narrow-hipped swimmer's body. The sleeves of his V-neck jersey—cashmere. she was convinced—were pushed halfway up tanned and muscled forearms. The fine material skimmed his wide chest and hugged big, muscular upper arms. He wore a pair of black trousers that didn't disguise the length and strength of his legs. Trendy black-and-white trainers covered his big feet and he carried an expensive-looking bag and a sleek laptop case.

He was breathtakingly, knee-shakingly sexy. *Hot.*

Lex was currently single and would be for the short- and, she presumed, medium-term future. Even if she had time for an affair—which she didn't—most men backed away when they realised her love life had to be scheduled around the needs and demands of her half-sisters. Even if it was just a short-term fling, men didn't like not being at the top of her priority list.

Even if she wanted a relationship—and she didn't—her mum had jumped in and out of relationships her entire life so she was cynical about love and humans' ability to commit—having a guy in her life would be impractical and unworkable.

Even a short-term affair would be tricky but, wow,

with someone like Gorgeous Guy she'd make the effort to fit him into her day. Or night.

He stopped, pulled a smart phone from the back pocket of his trousers and scowled down at it, his thick eyebrows pulling together. His hair was a rich, dark sable, cut short to keep the waves under control. She couldn't tell what colour his eyes were, but his nose was long, his jaw chiselled and his cheekbones high. He wasn't pretty-boy handsome but, man, his sheer masculinity stopped traffic. Lex grinned as a woman turned back to look at him, not watching where she was going, and bumped into a luggage trolley she hadn't noticed.

Lex didn't blame her. Gorgeous Guy deserved a second or third look.

Unable to look away, she watched as he raked his hand through his hair, obviously frustrated. He jabbed a finger at his phone and lifted it to his ear, scowling. He looked Italian—maybe Greek or Arabic? His nationality didn't matter. He would be classified as a hottie from Cartagena to Canberra and everywhere in between.

And she had to stop gawking at him before he noticed her open mouth and glassy eyes. Honestly, she should get out more if she was this affected by a random handsome guy in an airport terminal.

Pull yourself together, Satchell!

Unfortunately, yanking her eyes off him proved harder than she expected. She was about to—she was!—when he turned his head and his eyes collided with hers. Despite being across the room, she felt the heat of his gaze as his eyes moved over her face and down her long body. It was easy enough to figure out what he was thinking: bright-red hair, long and curly, tendrils springing out around a heart-shaped face, every inch covered in distinctive freckles with a small nose, a wide mouth and green eyes. A tallish, too-thin redhead dressed in black jeans, biker boots and a battered black denim jacket over a long-sleeved white T-shirt.

He didn't drop his eyes or walk away and a hot slap of attraction hit her, causing the world to shift under her feet. A million tiny needles hit her over-sensitised skin and she felt light-headed and weird. Why did all the colours and sounds in the airport seem amplified? Maybe she was having a stroke because all her nerve endings felt as if they were on fire, sending bolts of current up her arms and straight to her heart.

Or maybe this was pure animal attraction. She tipped her head to the side. She'd heard of the phenomenon but had never experienced it, not to this degree anyway. He picked up his overnight bag and started to walk...

And, good grief, was he heading in her direction? Was he seriously going to initiate a conversation... with her? What? *Why?*

She was way out of practice with guys and didn't know how to flirt any more. Lex shuffled from foot to foot, her heartbeat loud in her ears. She couldn't get enough air into her lungs and, despite having taken a few sips of icy coffee, her mouth felt as if it hadn't experienced liquid for weeks. What would he say when he reached her. How would she respond? Lex darted a quick look over her shoulder… Maybe someone behind her had captured his attention and she was reading the situation wrong, but…nope. He was definitely focused on her.

And, standing in a busy airport, she felt naked, emotionally vulnerable. As if he knew her or could easily discover her secrets. That he knew that, beneath her insouciant exterior and her 'I've got this handled' attitude, she was floundering and second-guessing everything she did.

And, sometimes, who she was.

Damn, he was still heading her way, his eyes still locked on her face. Why couldn't she look away from him? What was wrong with her?

As he approached, Lex realised his eyes were a topaz-brown colour, a gorgeous mixture of gold and amber tinged with hints of green. Lex, feeling off-balance and more than a little shocked—he was now just a few feet from her—felt her sign fall to the floor. His cologne, a masculine combination of sandalwood, lime and something herby, drifted over to her, along with the hint of expensive soap. He'd showered recently because the tips of his wavy hair were wet, but he hadn't bothered to shave, as thick stubble covered his lower face.

Up close he was even more impressive than he was from a distance and Lex tightened the grip on her coffee cup.

Be cool, Lex. Don't do, or say, anything stupid.

Lex tipped her head back to look up into his eyes as he opened his mouth to speak.

'I'm Cole Thorpe...'

But, before he could finish his sentence, a loud jangle emanated from the back pocket of her jeans, causing her to jump. The ring sounded like a foghorn—she'd made it that loud so she could hear it ring from every corner of the house—and Lex squeezed her plastic coffee cup so hard that the lid popped off. She watched, horrified, as a long stream of cold coffee flew into that hard face and down that wide, cashmere-covered chest.

Oh.

Oh, *help!*

Cole was used to walking off his private jet and straight into a car that would whisk him away to his next destination, a seamless transition that he'd made five hundred times or more. His arrival in Cape Town had been anything but standard.

And, so far, deeply annoying.

Had his long-term virtual PA been in charge of his travel arrangements, he would already be in a car, halfway to Thorpe Industries, Cape Town. But, because Gary was on paternity leave, Cole was making do with another virtual assistant he'd found through some agency. So far she was proving to be a shade up from useless. In capitals. And by the end of the day, if he remembered, she'd be gone and he'd be onto temporary assistant number four. He had too many balls in the air for inefficiency and needed someone who could make his life easier, not harder. And, really, what was so difficult about making sure he had a ride from the airport to Thorpe Industries' Cape Town headquarters?

After hanging around in the airport for fifteen minutes—a complete waste of time—he'd reached someone at Thorpe Industries who'd told him that the driver's instructions were to wait at International Arrivals. She had a sign, he was told, but you couldn't miss her...

His driver was a woman, and would probably be dressed in black. She also had red hair. Once he started looking for her, Cole found her almost immediately, only to find her eyes already on him. For the first time, his feet felt glued to the floor and his lungs didn't seem to be taking in enough air.

She was tall, maybe five-eight in those clunky, ugly boots, but to say that she had red hair would be like saying the sun was yellow. It was a deeply unimaginative description for such an unusual shade. Long and curly, it wasn't red, orange or auburn, but a cacophony of colours, reminding him of the fallen maple leaves that carpeted the ground at the end of autumn in the Bukhansan National Park in South Korea. And those freckles...

They ranged from pinpricks to tiny dots, each one perfect. Hers wasn't just a spray across her nose, or on her cheeks, but her entire face was covered in a Milky Way of cinnamon-coloured tiny stars.

Heart-stopping stunning.

Her hair and her freckles captured his attention—

how could they not? Her body was slim but curvy, and she had dark-red, perfectly arched eyebrows over bright eyes—green or blue?—and a wide, sexy mouth. Without her freckles and red hair, she'd be another attractive woman, but her unusual colouring made her stand out from the crowd. And that wasn't easy in a busy airport.

She was also, apparently and weirdly, his driver. Cole looked down at the sign she held in her hand— it was upside down—and winced internally. She was the first woman he'd been attracted to in months— the last six months had been hectic and his sex life had dropped way down his list of priorities—and she worked as a driver for Thorpe Industries.

He didn't play where he worked. Ever.

Tucking his phone into the back pocket of his jeans, he swung his bag up so that it hung off his shoulder and started to wind his way through the crowds to the redhead. She watched him approach, her eyes wary. Then her lips parted and her tongue appeared between strong, very white teeth. He was old enough and experienced enough to know that his immediate, and intensely inconvenient, attraction to her was reciprocated.

After everything that had happened these past few months, this was not what he needed.

Slowing down, Cole told himself to take a breath, to gain control. He was tired, stressed, overworked and he was overreacting. She was just another woman, nobody special. He didn't believe in special and he didn't have time for an affair. He had a hedge fund to manage, a company he didn't want to sell and a life to resume.

He'd be in and out of Cape Town in a week... maybe two.

Forcing his feet to move, Cole walked towards his driver, telling his stomach to unknot, his throat to loosen and his lungs to take a breath. He couldn't let her know that he found her compelling, let her suspect that it felt as if she'd slid her hand through his ribs and held his heart in a tight grip.

Normally very cool and completely collected, Cole had never been sideswiped by attraction before, and he was stumbling around in unknown territory. But he only had a few feet to pull himself together...

Three, two, one...

He took his final steps up to her and introduced himself, only to be interrupted by the sound of a foghorn piercing a dark, stormy night. He braked, the redhead squeezed her takeaway container of coffee and a stream of the cold, sticky liquid hit his cheek and lips and slid off his chin to fall to his chest and then the floor.

He stood there, shocked and, well, wet, wondering what else could go wrong. Then tears started to roll down the redhead's face.

He could handle a long flight, being inconvenienced, having to track down his ride and being smacked in the gut by a very unexpected attraction... but a woman's tears?

Nope. They were enough to drop him to the floor.

* * *

As her phone went silent, Lex closed her eyes, praying that this was a nightmare, that she hadn't just started crying in front of her boss, the brand-new owner of Thorpe Industries, the man who, indirectly but ultimately, signed off on her pay cheques.

What on earth was wrong with her? She never cried. Why in front of him? And why right now?

Lex scrabbled in her tote bag for a pack of tissues and pulled out a small pack, her shaking fingers unable to pull back the tab to the opening. A tanned hand gently took the packet and pulled back the tab, allowing her to pull a couple of tissues from the pack. She wiped her eyes, thankful she seldom wore make-up. Streaks of mascara down her cheeks did not pair well with wet eyes and the post-box-red of her skin under her freckles.

Oh, how she longed for the floor to cave in beneath her feet. Anything would be preferable to standing here, feeling like a complete, over-emotional wreck. The last time she'd spontaneously cried was when Joelle had bleached her hair and she'd ended up looking like a half-ripe apricot. She'd been thirteen. She was now more than double that age and should be in control of her emotions.

The problem was that she normally was.

So why was she crying? What was wrong with her? She'd known sad, and she was a long way off from feeling that overwhelming emotion. Sure, she was tired, but she'd learned to function on minimal sleep. Was she stressed?

She was a woman in her late twenties trying, with the help of her sister Addi, to raise her young half-sisters, study, stretch their income further than it was supposed to go and keep their rag-tag family together. She was studying psychology. She knew that stress always found a way to express itself, sometimes when the person was least expecting it. It rolled through the body, looking for a way out, and sometimes it was released through tears.

And exhaustion inhibited the body's ability to self-regulate and made it more prone to emotional outbursts. Yes, she tended to shove her feelings down, telling herself she didn't have time to deal with them, that she'd process all she was feeling later when she was less tired, when she was alone. However, she never had time, was infrequently alone and there was a good chance that all those pesky feelings had piled on top of each other and spilt over and out.

But why did she have to cry in front of Cole Thorpe, her boss? Was it because, subconsciously at least, her attraction to him made her realise that she was still a woman, still capable of feeling sexually aroused and knowing there wasn't a damn thing she could do about it, even if she'd wanted to? Was it because seeing him, knowing that she couldn't just accept a potential offer to join him for a drink or dinner later, made her remember all she'd sacrificed for her sisters, all that she couldn't have?

Had it made her see that she wasn't a normal single woman, that she had more responsibilities than most, that she sometimes felt trapped, and felt guilty for feeling that way?

Possibly. Probably.

She could figure out the reasons for her tears later—they were so stupid!—but right now she needed to rescue this situation, preferably before Cole Thorpe fired her. If he did that, she'd have a very decent excuse to cry and another huge reason to stress. She desperately needed this job: it worked around her big sister-substitute mum duties.

Lex sniffed and lifted her eyes to see a black jersey being pulled up to reveal a washboard stomach and a muscled chest. Her mouth fell open as a steady hum started in her womb and the space between her legs buzzed, getting warmer by the second.

His sweater came off and he impatiently tugged down the black T-shirt that had ridden up his chest. She couldn't help noticing his bulging arms as he dragged his jersey over his coffee-splashed face and chest. Then he dropped to his haunches, snapped open his leather bag and pulled out another sweater, pale-grey this time, and pulled it over his head. He shoved the black jersey into a corner of his bag and stood up.

From start to finish, his swapping of jerseys couldn't have taken more than a minute, but Lex felt as if she'd watched the longest, sexiest movie in her life. And she wanted to hit rewind.

He was her boss, and Lex needed to stay employed, so maybe, instead of ogling him, she should apologise profusely and try and act like the professional she knew she could be. But, after having shared some serious eye contact, tossed her coffee over him and burst into tears, there was a good chance that she might have over-cooked her golden goose.

Lex held out her hand, gave him an embarrassed smile and cleared her throat. 'I'm sorry. For tossing coffee over you and crying.'

He put his hand in hers and gave it the briefest shake before dropping it as if it was a Cape Cobra. 'And you are?'

She'd forgotten to give him her name. *Great.* 'I'm Lex Satchell.'

He nodded, picked up his overnight bag and slung it over his shoulder. 'I've seen enough of this airport, so I'd like to get out of here. Where's the car?'

It was hard to think around him. 'Uh, we need to go down a floor. It's not far but, if you prefer, you can wait in the pick-up zone. I'll take your bag to the car.'

'I've got legs. I can walk.'

He had very nice, very long, very strong legs… *Stop it, Lex!*

'Let's go,' he added, his tone brusque. 'I want to check in at my hotel and drop in at Thorpe's Cape Town headquarters today.'

So did that mean she wasn't fired? Or was he just waiting for her to deliver him to wherever he wanted to go before he canned her? Lex started to ask him but he took off towards the escalator, moving quickly.

Lex followed his broad shoulders, feeling dazed and disoriented. He was implacable and unreadable, and she suspected she wasn't the first, and certainly wouldn't be the last, person who'd wonder which way was up around the inscrutable international businessman.

CHAPTER TWO

COLE SAT IN the back seat of the Thorpe Industries SUV, diagonally behind his sexy driver—his *driver*, Cole mentally reminded himself—dark sunglasses over his eyes. He had to stop looking at her, but his eyes kept bouncing from her lovely profile to her slim shoulder, to the one hand he could see on the steering wheel. She drove with cool competence, easily manoeuvring the big car in busy traffic. Her eyes darted between the rear view and side mirrors, and he found it hard to believe that the cool, remote woman behind the wheel was the same one who'd been crying just twenty minutes before.

Judging by the mortification in her green eyes, crying wasn't something she did often. Or at all. What had set her off? They'd been trading glances, and he'd seen the awareness of him in her eyes. He'd introduced himself, her phone had rung and she'd tossed coffee over him. Had she been scared he'd yell at her, lash out at her, fire her? Was that what had caused her to become emotional?

His curiosity burned a hole in his stomach lining,

and he fought to keep the urge to demand an explanation behind his teeth. She was his employee. He had no right to that knowledge and the best way to show her respect was to pretend nothing had happened.

But he couldn't. Partly, yeah, because of that curiosity—an anomaly in itself, because people generally weren't interesting enough for him to dive into their psyche—and partly because he wanted to comfort her, to make everything that upset her go away.

The urge to take her in his arms and shield her from the world terrified him. He'd never been protected, and even as a child he'd been expected to take, and deal with, life's vagaries, disappointments and lack of fairness. He didn't coddle people—didn't know how—so his need to protect and remedy whatever ailed her confounded him.

Cole swallowed his sigh and turned his head to look out of the window, catching a glimpse of a low-income suburb on the side of the road. He was now in the southernmost city in Africa, last week he'd been in Chicago, two weeks before he'd been in Hong Kong. As well as visiting Thorpe Industries' regional offices, he was also managing his internationally acclaimed, billion-dollar hedge fund.

His candle was now a stub the size of a thumb nail.

Cole slipped his index finger and thumb under his sunglasses and pushed them into his closed eyelids, and an image of his older brother meditating in his orange robes flashed behind his eyes.

Did Sam ever think about crisscrossing the world in the Thorpe private jet, wearing five-thousand-dollar suits or the long work days and the responsibility of being the CEO of Thorpe Industries demanded? He'd walked away from his privileged life of being the highly educated, driven, feted first-born son of Grenville Thorpe—the famous industrialist—to join a Buddhist monastery and Cole wondered if he regretted his decision.

Cole dropped his fingers and opened his eyes, but the events of the past six months rolled through his mind in a series of snapshots. His father's death a year ago had been a shock, not because Cole felt any grief for the man he'd never known, but because Grenville dying of a heart attack had put a mortal dent in his plans to take revenge on the father who'd ignored him all his life.

For five years before Grenville's death, or more, he'd been quietly and surreptitiously buying up Thorpe Industries shares and had amassed a big block of shares in the multinational company his father had owned and operated. He'd been a few months off staging a hostile takeover—his father wouldn't have been able to ignore him or that—when Grenville had died of a heart attack on his yacht off the Amalfi coast. Sam, his brother, had inherited all of Grenville's assets and Grenville's shares in Thorpe Industries.

Cole, unsurprisingly, hadn't been mentioned in the will.

Since Cole hadn't had the same desire to ruin Sam as he had Grenville, he'd stepped back and reevaluated his plans. His only aim in acquiring Thorpe shares had been to look his father in the eye as he'd told him that he'd no longer be ignored or dismissed.

But death had whipped his revenge out of his hands.

Then Sam, on the six-month anniversary of their father's death, had swapped his Armani suits for orange robes, his single life as one of the world's most eligible bachelors for abstinence, and material abundance for one meal a day and sleeping on a thin mat, covered only by his robes. Cole had had no problem with Sam reinventing his life—that was his choice—but what had possessed Sam to transfer every asset he owned, and everything he'd inherited from Grenville, including his controlling interest in Thorpe Industries, to Cole? How dared he? What on earth had his brother been thinking?

Cole would have asked him but Sam, according to his London-based lawyer and point of contact, was currently unavailable. Sam was fine. He stood by his decision to transfer everything to Cole, he had no interest in the outside world and was living his best life.

Cole had wanted the company, the lawyer said, so Sam had given it to him.

Yeah, but he hadn't wanted Thorpe Industries like this—it meant nothing without the sweet taste of revenge. Now it was, simply, a pain in his backside.

Cole flipped his phone over and over, thinking that Grenville had to be doing cartwheels in his grave. His worshipped firstborn—not an exaggeration—had renounced everything, including his name, and his despised and shunned second-born son now owned all his worldly possessions. Despised? No, that was wrong. You had to care about someone or something to despise them, Grenville hadn't been able to gather enough energy to hate him. He'd been discounted and discarded, not worthy of his father's notice.

Cole's phone buzzed and he looked down at the screen, sighing when he saw the identity of the caller. He ignored the call and allowed it to go to voice mail. Somehow, along with his company, apartments and all his material possessions, Cole had also inherited the responsibility of Sam's long-term girlfriend, Melissa. He now owned the aristocratic blonde's apartment and he'd continued Sam's tradition of paying her a hefty monthly allowance.

Cole didn't mind her having the apartment and cash. She and Sam had been together for a long time and she'd expected to marry him some day. She deserved some sort of compensation for the trauma his brother had put her through. But, over the last couple of months, despite sharing nothing more than a few dinners and attending a mutual friend's wedding together, the press had started linking them together, treating them like a couple.

Not on, Cole decided. He'd had a couple of serious relationships in his early and mid-twenties, all of which had fizzled away. He wasn't good at being part of a couple, he pushed people away when they asked for emotional intimacy. He'd been raised by an unemotional mother, had been ignored by his father and had had little contact with his brother. He was better on his own, was used to his solitary life, and when he got back to London he'd present Melissa with an exit package of a couple of million and ownership of the flat. That would ease the sting of severing her ties to the Thorpe family.

Hopefully, getting rid of Thorpe Industries would be as easy. Early on, he'd decided that dismantling the company and selling its assets to local business people was the most logical and efficient way to rid himself of the Thorpe empire.

While he could get a lot from spreadsheets and balance sheets, Cole knew that the best way to gather information was to get his boots on the ground, to make his own assessments. He'd spent many weeks crisscrossing the world, visiting all Thorpe companies and inspecting the assets he'd received from Sam. He'd put Sam's London and Hong Kong apartments on the market, sold his yacht and private helicopter and his art collection was due to be sold at auction in a few months. Cole intended to put a portion of the proceeds he realised into a fixed-term investment in case Sam decided he didn't want to be a monk any more, but the rest he intended to distribute to various charities. He had his own apartments, art and car collections—he wasn't into yachts—and he didn't need his brother's pass-me-downs. He had enough of his own money. He didn't need Sam's or his father's.

His African assets were fairly straightforward and he didn't foresee any complications.

Lex looked in the rear-view mirror and caught Cole's bleak expression—she should think of him as Mr

Thorpe but, because she'd seen his ridged stomach and his bare chest, she couldn't. She wished she could ask him what was bothering him, why he looked as if he carried the weight of the world resting on his impressively wide shoulders.

He looked so damn lonely…

Despite knowing it wasn't her place—drivers didn't speak to owners of companies—Lex knew she was going to say something, although she knew not what. All she knew was that she was desperate to distract him and needed to pull him back from whatever dark place he'd wandered into. It wasn't her place or part of her duties, and he might tell her to mind her own business, but nobody should look that…that *desolate*.

But she already had two black marks against her—tossing coffee and crying—and she didn't want to give him an excuse to hand her another one, so her question couldn't be personal. So, what should she say? Ah, just around the next bend was a decent view of Table Mountain: she could point it out and ask him if he'd visited Cape Town before. The city was an innocuous, friendly subject.

Cole Thorpe, despite having all the money in the world—that was a limited-edition luxury watch on his wrist—looked as though he needed a friend.

Lex was about to speak when her phone rang. She expected it to be the receptionist at Thorpe Industries again—her call precipitated the Toss Coffee Over Your Boss incident—but, when she looked down, Lex recognised the number of St Agnes primary school and her heart lurched. Getting a call from her half-sisters' school was never good.

If the call had come from anyone else, she would've ignored it, but a call from the girls' school shot her anxiety levels sky-high. She answered the call via Bluetooth, knowing that Cole would hear the conversation. Damn, another black mark. She was racking them up today.

Within twenty seconds she established that the girls were fine but Nixi's teacher was calling to remind Lex that she'd promised to supply the school with twenty-four cupcakes for their bake sale.

'And we need them here by lunchtime,' she was told.

Cupcakes? What cupcakes?

'I'm sorry, what cupcakes?' Lex demanded, her stomach sinking to her toes. The school frequently made last-minute requests—or, truthfully, she processed the necessary information late—but two hours to produce two-dozen cupcakes was terrifying on another level.

'I sent a reminder a week ago.'

Lex winced. Yeah, her inbox was full to overflowing and she could easily have missed it. 'Look, I dropped the ball,' she told Ms Mapton. 'Even if I could get to a bakery to buy them, I don't think I'll be able to get them to you in time.'

'Just do your best, Ms Satchell,' Ms Mapton told her before disconnecting the call.

She'd try but she didn't see how she'd fit a cupcake delivery into her day. She didn't know whether Cole needed her to ferry him around any more today and, if he did, she'd have to postpone her French lesson student. She also had an assignment to email off before five this afternoon, as yet unfinished. But Cole's claim on her time came first: her part-time chauffeuring gig for Thorpe Industries, which she'd acquired through Addi, paid well and it wasn't one she could afford to lose.

That was if he didn't fire her today.

Lex turned her attention back to her cupcake problem. How had she dropped this ball? If she didn't deliver the cupcakes, she knew her sisters would be disappointed, which would be quickly followed by resigned acceptance. Snow and Nixi were so used to being disappointed by Joelle, the mother all five sisters shared, that being let down wasn't anything new or strange.

Cupcakes. What else was this day going to throw at her?

Lex slipped the SUV into the fast lane to overtake a fuel truck. She considered calling Addi, who worked at Thorpe in the hospitality section, but knew her older sister was in meetings all day and wouldn't take her call. She'd ordinarily ask Addi's assistant Giles, who was also a family friend, to do the cupcake run, but she couldn't—not with their boss of bosses listening in.

She didn't want to paint a bullseye on Addi's back because it was her job that paid the bulk of their joint expenses while Lex provided the day-to-day care the younger girls needed. Without each other's contribution, the younger girls would've been split apart and placed in the foster care system, because neither she nor Addi could look after them on their own. Addi's salary made it financially possible for them to stay together, and Lex being present for the girls gave them the emotional stability neither she nor Addi had had growing up. But, lately, because Addi went to work early and walked in late, Lex frequently felt like a single parent.

She couldn't believe so much time had passed since they'd taken responsibility for the girls. At twenty-three, she'd been single, and she'd just met someone she thought might be the one to change her mind about love, trust and commitment. Addi had been engaged, counting down to her wedding in three months, and Storm, their middle sister, had just left school. Then, after not hearing a word from their mother in seven years, Joelle had rocked up with Nixi and Snow—sisters they'd never met, sisters they hadn't known about. She and Addi had been busy taking in that bombshell news—Joelle now had five daughters from five different men—when Joelle had asked them to look after the girls for a weekend.

They were still waiting for Joelle to return to the country.

As a result of Joelle's daughter-dump, Addi's wedding had been postponed and then cancelled. Lex's love interest had done a runner and, yet again, her suspicion that 'love' always melted when came into contact with a little heat was confirmed. Addi's father had bolted when Joelle had told him she was pregnant with Addi—Lex didn't even know who her dad was. Joelle invariably skipped out on a person or situation when times got tough, and Addi's fiancé had broken up with her just two months after their half-sisters' arrival in their lives.

She got the message: love couldn't be counted on to see you through the tough times. Determination, persistence and grit were the traits needed to deal with the reality of a stunningly fickle mum and raising her two half-sisters.

Love was outstandingly unreliable and, frankly, useless.

The onboard GPS broke into her thoughts by telling her to take the next exit and Lex shook herself out of her introspective reverie. She was normally too busy to look back, and she rarely allowed herself to think of the past and the rough hand she and Addi had been dealt. It was what it was, and no amount of thinking, or wishing, could change reality.

Enough now. She was tired and stressed and that was why she was being bombarded with memories of the past. And, at twenty-eight, she couldn't operate on three hours of sleep night after night and be expected to be Positive Polly.

Two more years of studying, she told herself as she took the exit. Then she'd have her degree in Forensic Psychology and, with the girls being a little older, she could look for a full-time job. She could maybe even think about having a fling, some fun.

Until then, she just had to keep trying her best. It was all she could do. But sometimes Lex felt that her best wasn't nearly good enough and she was letting her sisters down, just like her mother had let her down, time and time again. But she, at least, was showing up, climbing into the ring, doing her best.

She was doing all she could, in the best way she knew how. All she could do was keep putting one foot in front of the other and trudging on.

'Do you have kids?'

Lex looked in the rear-view mirror and her stomach flipped over when her eyes connected with Cole's. Was that disappointment she saw? No, she was just projecting her attraction onto him. Rich, handsome guys who operated in nose-bleedingly high social circles didn't waste their time, energy or emotions on women who were anything less than stunningly beautiful or incredibly talented—possibly both.

But his question broke the tense silence between them and for that she was grateful. 'No, the cupcakes are for a bake sale at my sisters' school.'

'And why did you get the call? Where's their mum?'

Lex stopped at a traffic light and her grip on the steering wheel tightened. 'Me and my sister Addi—she works as a VP at Thorpe in your hospitality and leisure sector—are raising our half-sisters together.'

She saw what she thought might be respect, possibly approval, flit across his face. 'Did one or both of your parents die?'

Their deaths would have been so much easier to explain than Joelle's deep selfishness and lack of responsibility. The traffic light turned green, Lex accel-

erated and slammed on the brakes when a passenger
bus cut in front of her, far too close for comfort. She
hit her horn, the bus accelerated away and a brief
wave was the only apology she got.

'Cape Town drivers are the worst,' she told Cole,
seeing the stone gates for the Vane Hotel up ahead.
'But we are nearly there.'

'Pity,' Cole murmured.

And what, Lex wondered as she steered the car
through the gates to the Vane, did he mean by that
cryptic statement?

CHAPTER THREE

LEX DROVE UP the winding drive to the Vane Hotel and Cole immediately noticed the city's famous mountain behind the sprawling hotel, now understanding why it was said the Vane had the best views of Table Mountain. Despite Thorpe Industries owning a boutique hotel on the Waterfront, Jude Fisher, who was a friend of the owners, had recommended this hotel to him, saying that, in a city that boasted incredible hotels such as the Silo and Mount Nelson, the Vane was the best of the best, boasting six-star elegance and facilities, and staying there was an experience not be missed.

Lex pulled up under the portico and Cole released the catch to his seatbelt and pushed a hand through his hair. He was about to exit the car when Lex hit the button to drop her window and asked the valet to give her a minute. The valet hesitated, nodded and stepped back.

Lex turned round in her seat and her extraordinary eyes slammed into his. 'Are you intending to go to Thorpe Industries today? Shall I wait, or when should I return?'

He shook his head, recalling her question. 'My assistant has organised a hire car for me. I prefer to drive myself,' he told her, desperately trying to ignore the prickle of attraction flying up and down his spine. Maybe he could cancel the car and get Lex to drive him round Cape Town. He loathed not being behind the wheel but wouldn't mind spending more time looking at her unusual but gorgeous face.

It was an idea...

It was an asinine one. He'd long held the belief that having a driver was both pretentious and a waste of money since he could drive himself wherever he needed to go. And being in the close confines of a car with someone he wanted more than he needed to breathe was a recipe for disaster.

She was his employee, for goodness' sake. He didn't cross that line—ever. That was asking for complications he didn't need or have time for. But the thought of not seeing her again while he was in Cape Town was a knife through his temple, a kick to his head.

He wanted to know why she was raising her sisters, and how that had come to be. He wanted to taste the skin on her neck, kiss his way down her spine and hook her naked thigh over his hip. He wanted...

Seriously, Thorpe? Cole took the opportunity to run his hands up and down his face, trying to wake up his brain cells. What was wrong with him? And what was it about this woman that fascinated him so?

He'd known many beautiful, stunning women, and had slept with quite a few of them, but none of them made him feel as if he were sixteen again, disconcerted and enthralled.

She's just another woman...

He could repeat that mantra until the sun rose in the morning, but it wouldn't make a jot of difference. There was, as they said, something about her that called to him on a deep and dark—scary—level.

And that, more than anything, was why he had to stay away from her. 'So you won't need me to drive you anywhere?'

'No.' Unfortunately.

He thought he saw disappointment flash in her eyes, possibly panic, and was tempted to change his mind, to put up with the frustration of being driven simply to see her again. Maybe the time difference and jet lag were messing with his mind and his emotions. Then Cole silently cursed when he remembered that he'd got a solid six hours of sleep last night as the plane had flown south and that there was only a two-hour time difference between London and Cape Town.

But those eyes in that face, and her raspy, deep voice, enthralled him. He could look at her, listen to her, for the longest time.

A porter and a car valet approached them and Cole exited the vehicle, with Lex half a second behind him. He saw a well-dressed woman exit from the lobby and knew she was his personal concierge. He was about to thank and dismiss Lex when his phone rang, the call coming in being from one of his biggest investor clients. She wasn't someone whose call he could ignore.

He looked at Lex and nodded to the concierge. 'Tell her who I am and grab my laptop bag from the boot and take it up to my room. Wait with it until I get there.' His state-of-the-art laptop was his life and he never let it out of his sight. It held all his personal, business and client information, yet he instinctively trusted Lex to transport it to his room.

Of course, he could've just held it while he took his call. It wasn't as if it was heavy. Not wanting to interrogate that thought, he turned away and answered his call.

Ten minutes later he stepped into the impressive art deco style lobby, the concierge approached him and offered to show him to his room. He took his hotel card, asked for directions to the penthouse suite and declined her company. It was a hotel suite, not interstellar travel.

On the top floor, in the east corner, he stepped into a hallway and saw Lex standing in the open door to his suite, his laptop bag over her shoulder. On hearing his footsteps, the porter appeared in the doorway, a polite smile on his face. 'Would you like me to unpack for you, Mr Thorpe?'

Cole slipped him a tip and told him that he'd manage. When the porter was out of sight, Cole looked at Lex and stepped inside the hallway to his suite, his eyes drifting over the sophisticated lounge to the massive windows dominating the space. His room was high up, so he looked over old oak trees directly at Table Mountain.

'That's got to be the best view in Cape Town.'

He turned to see Lex standing next to him in the hall, her eyes on the view. He'd never been to the city before, but he thought she might be right. It would be hard to beat.

After another minute of silence, with both of them looking at the incredible view, he turned back to face Lex. She'd transferred his laptop bag to her hand, and he reached for it, their fingers brushing. Cole couldn't believe that such a small touch could hold so much power, and he tensed, unable to pull his eyes off her truly lovely face. Her green eyes darkened and underneath the freckles he saw a pink flush, some distinct heat in her cheeks. The tip of her pink tongue touched her upper lip and she rocked on her feet...

'Mr Thorpe, I...' She started to speak but her words faded when she noticed their fingers entangled as they both gripped the handle of his laptop bag. She stared down at their hands, but she didn't pull away, as he'd expected her to.

He should break the contact now...immediately. She was his driver, his employee, someone he should not be this close to—ever. But he could no more break their contact than he could stop his heart from beating.

'You should move back,' he told her, his voice rough-sounding.

'I should,' she agreed, sounding bemused and dazed. 'I want to, I know I must, but I can't.'

He released a groan and inhaled a solid hit of her scent, something fresh and unisex, light and lovely. Instead of pulling away, his thumb slid over her knuckles. Passion flared in her eyes, her breath hitched and she tipped her head back, lifting her mouth. What else could he do but lower his mouth to hers?

He was an inch from her mouth, and anticipation hummed through his veins, when she slapped her hand on her chest and pulled back. His eyes connected with hers and he saw panic and a healthy dose of anxiety.

'Are you married?' she demanded.

'No.'

'Engaged, seeing someone, sleeping with someone?' she demanded.

He hadn't had sex in months. He'd been too busy to think about taking a woman to bed. The only woman he had any contact with on a personal level was Melissa, but there had never been anything between them. Okay, they'd kissed once, but that had been at her instigation, not his. She was connected to him through Sam, not because he wanted her in his life.

'No,' he told Lex, desperate to taste her.

'Are you sure about that?'

'Yes, damn it. Can I kiss you now?'

'We shouldn't. I work for you,' Lex told him, the expression on her face yearning. She wanted his mouth on hers as much as he wanted his there. If he pressed her, he knew she'd admit that their attraction, their desperation to see each other naked, was all that was important right now.

'Tell me not to kiss you, Cole,' Lex begged.

'I can't,' he whispered, bending his knees a little to meet her mouth.

He was about to make contact when voices coming from the passage—there were two penthouse suites—pulled him back to the present. The door to the suite was open and anyone walking past would get more than an eyeful. Cole stepped away from Lex and a cold dose of reality slapped him in the face. He was in Cape Town to work—Lex was his driver, for goodness' sake.

He didn't do this. He wasn't the type of guy who hit on female employees, not if they were directors, managers or cleaners—or chauffeurs.

He owned the company. He paid her salary.

He. Wasn't. That. Guy.

At the sound of the lift door opening behind him in the hallway, Cole dropped to his haunches to pick up his laptop bag.

As three people passed his open door, he turned his back to them and gripped the handle of the laptop bag, hauling in long, deep gulps of winter air.

'Thanks for the lift,' he told Lex.

She nodded. He noticed that her braid was loose, and he wondered how it would look spread out on his pillow. 'It's my job.'

He took a deep breath and she nodded once before turning away and walking down the hallway to the lift. When the lift doors closed, he bent over and put his hands on his thighs, bent over and took a couple of long, steadying breaths. He couldn't remember when he'd last felt so shaky and off-balance.

How—in the name of all things holy—had things got out of hand so quickly?

Before her younger sisters had arrived, Lex had had a lover or two and thought she knew what attraction was.

She'd been so very, very wrong...

She liked men, liked how they made her feel, but nothing prepared her for the intensity she and Cole shared. As soon as his fingers connected with hers, she'd felt as if she was being tugged towards a portal and, had he kissed her, he would've propelled her into another universe where nothing existed but them.

Despite their non-kiss, she still felt shaky, off-balance and, hours later, her heart was still bouncing off the walls of her ribcage. A million butterflies had taken up residence in her stomach and she felt as though she could sleep for a week or run an ultra-marathon.

In other words, she didn't feel like herself.

Lex stood on the small veranda off the lounge of Addi's and her cottage, a blanket wrapped around her shoulders, the laughter of her sisters drifting in from where they were gathered in the kitchen. As they did every few minutes, her thoughts drifted back to what might've happened in the hotel room. Alone with Cole, she'd been oblivious to anything but him, entranced by the desire in his warm eyes, desperate to feel his mouth on hers, his big hands moving over her body.

When he looked at her, he made her feel powerful. Feminine. Lovely.

After she'd walked away from him, and when her heart rate had dropped to a pace where she thought it wasn't about to explode, she'd left the lift and taken a slow walk through the hotel to where the valet had delivered the SUV, hoping that the freezing wind would cool her burning cheeks and shock her back to reality. It hadn't, and for the rest of the day she'd been less than useless.

And she'd completely forgotten about the cupcakes... Snow and Nixi were still unimpressed.

Lex sighed, pulled her blanket tighter around her shoulders and sat down on the sofa tucked under the eaves. She pulled her legs up and rested her cheek on her knee, feeling both tired and, oh, so wired. Up until today, she hadn't known how intense physical attraction could be, how it could cause one to act irrationally. If she'd had any warning of the way Cole would flip her inside out, she would've run a mile, because she was very familiar with the effects of unbridled desire: she'd been living with the fallout of it all her life.

Her mother Joelle was a very sensual woman, someone who never hid the fact that she loved men, loved the way they made her feel and that she was built for excitement, not monogamy. Joelle ran from man to man, chasing that constant sexual high. If what Lex had experienced with Cole was the same high

Joelle chased, then she sort of got it. Why wouldn't she want more of that as often as she could get it?

Lex didn't have a problem, per se, with how Joelle lived her life. She couldn't care less how many men she had, who she slept with and why. It was her body, her life, her choice...

But Lex hated the fact that she and her sisters were the random casualties of her mother's war against societal norms, being sexually constrained and being expected to stay in one place with one man. As young girls, she and Addi had been introduced to so many men and shunted into the spare bedroom of Joelle's latest boyfriend's flat, house or hovel. They'd keep their heads down and pretend to be invisible but within a few weeks, sometimes a few months, they'd be on the move again.

Only Storm's dad, Tom, bless him, had managed a few years before he'd called it quits with Joelle, taking Storm with him. After their split, life had continued as normal—a series of strange houses and strange men—until their mid-teens, when Joelle had convinced her Aunt Kate to allow Addi and her to stay with her for the long summer holidays, telling her aunt she had work in Thailand.

Joelle hadn't returned in the New Year and had only come back six months later. It was hard to tell who'd been happier—she and Addi, or Joelle—when Aunt Kate had informed Joelle that the sisters had a permanent home with her. But, thanks to years of instability and having experienced Joelle's rapid and impulsive decisions to move them on, Lex had known that anything and everything could change and had refused to get her hopes up only to have them come crashing down again.

It was only when she and Addi had inherited this, Aunt Kate's, house on her death shortly after Lex's twenty-first birthday that she'd felt that they had a permanent base and security, a place that was theirs. Nobody would ever again force them to move, kick them out or throw their stuff onto the pavement. They would never again be at the mercy of someone's charity, used as a bargaining piece to stay: *'You can't kick us out! I have children!'* Nor would they be blamed for the demise of another of Joelle's relationships: *'If I didn't have you two, he'd still love me.'*

Of course, history had repeated itself when Joelle had returned five years ago with two more daughters in tow.

Lex often thought about Joelle, how easily promises, plans and words of love tripped off her tongue.

The words came as freely as a stream flowed down a mountainous slope, yet she always walked away, every single time. Despite doing everything she could to become what Joelle wanted, from changing her hair colour and covering her freckles, her mum always walked away.

And, if her mother couldn't love her enough to stick around, how could she trust anyone else to?

'Lex? Are you okay?'

Lex lifted her head to see Addi standing in the doorway to their sitting room, her ultra-short blonde hair ruffled. She carried a wine glass and handed it to Lex, before sitting down next to her. Lex pulled the blanket from her shoulders and draped it across their legs, snuggling up to her older sister. They'd spent their childhood like this, cleaved together, standing up to a world ruled by volatile adults and trying to follow rules they didn't understand.

'Are the girls watching TV?' Lex asked.

'Yes,' Addi answered. 'Are you okay? You've been out here for a while.'

'I...' Lex started to tell Addi about the almost-kiss, but stopped when she realised she was drinking alone. Sharing a glass at the end of a day was what they did, a tradition.

'Are you okay?' Lex asked. Now that she looked closely, Addi looked exhausted. She had blue circles under her eyes, her pale skin was tight across her cheekbones and her normally quick-to-smile mouth was full of tension. 'Have you heard anything about your job?'

Addi shook her head and Lex could see she didn't want to discuss her work situation. 'You know I'm not that worried if I get retrenched, Lex. Just last month I had two calls from companies wanting to headhunt me. I'll pick up something very quickly. Let's not talk about that now, okay?' Addi rested her temple on Lex's shoulder. 'Storm called and she wanted to know how we felt about her taking the girls with her to visit Hamish and Callie at a beach house they've rented in Durban for the upcoming winter holidays.'

Hamish was Storm's older half-brother by her father Tom's first marriage and was married to Nixi's and Snow's paediatrician. They had two sons, roughly the same ages as Nixi and Snow.

'And how do you feel about that?' Lex asked her.

'I think they should go,' Addi told her. 'Durban is divine in winter, so much warmer than here. The kids will have a blast. And who better to look after them than an orthopaedic surgeon, a paediatrician and their sister, who is an experienced au pair? And you need a break, Lex. You are exhausted.'

She was, and the thought of not having to worry about the girls for three weeks made her feel both guilty and thoroughly over-excited. 'I'm okay with them going,' she told Addi.

Lex placed her glass on the table next to her, not really in the mood for wine, trying to think of a way to introduce Cole Thorpe into their conversation. For some stupid reason she didn't understand, she wanted to know whether Addi had met Cole yet and what she thought of him.

'So I picked the big boss up earlier...' she said, silently cursing herself. Why was she torturing herself like this? She should just put him out of her mind. 'I tossed my coffee over him.'

Addi looked horrified. 'Oh, Lex! Please tell me you're joking?'

She wished. 'You're friendly with Trish in Human Resources, Ads. Have you heard that I'm going to be fired?'

'No, as far as I know, you're still on retainer as Thorpe's part-time driver.'

Okay, good. Phew.

'He's a good-looking guy,' Addi mused.

That was like saying an asteroid strike was a slap. 'Have you met him?' Lex asked, irritated by the hint of anxiety she heard in her voice. Addi was a brown-eyed blonde, completely ravishing, and men routinely fell over themselves to get her to notice them.

'He called a firm-wide staff meeting yesterday afternoon, introduced himself—told everyone that he's here to inspect the operation, to look at the assets and tour the companies under the Thorpe umbrella, to consider his options.'

'Did he mention selling?'

'No, but it's common knowledge that he's in negotiations in the US and in the East to sell those assets. He'll probably do the same here,' Addi stated, sounding calm. 'I think you should look for another part-time job, Lex.'

She had been, but there weren't many that paid as well and were as flexible as her Thorpe Industries gig.

'Why can't he just leave us alone?' Lex muttered. If he'd stayed in London, she wouldn't have to look for work again and she wouldn't be sitting here feeling jumpy, weird and out of sorts.

'There's weird tension in your voice every time you talk about him,' Addi commented.

You should see us together, Lex silently replied. Electricity hummed and the air shimmered.

'Did something happen while you were driving him?'

Her, 'No,' wasn't a lie. All that had happened in the car was that their eyes had occasionally collided in the mirror. She couldn't remember one thing about the drive from the airport to the CBD. It had been as if she'd been on autopilot. It was a miracle she hadn't crashed the car.

She never kept secrets from Addi but she couldn't tell her she and Cole had nearly kissed in his hotel room. She didn't understand it so she couldn't explain it.

She took an overlarge sip of her wine. Yes, he'd ignited a spark—or a raging fire—within her but it didn't mean anything. It couldn't. It was just one of those strange, inexplicably random things that happened that were never to be repeated. Their eyes had connected across a busy airport, she'd liked what she'd seen, and so had he. Lex skipped over the embarrassing memory of tossing coffee on him and her tears, pausing the movie playing in her head on the scene where he'd swapped his wet jersey for a dry one, giving her a super-quick peek of his simply marvellous, muscled, powerful torso.

And, yes, they'd indulged in some serious eye contact in the car—she'd never seen eyes his colour before, a light golden-brown—but after parking the SUV she'd pulled herself together and told herself to do her job. She'd done as he'd asked and had taken his laptop bag up to his penthouse suite, desperately thinking of how she could persuade him to let her drive him.

Then their fingers had touched—their *fingers* for goodness' sake!—and all hell had nearly broken loose.

Or heaven. Or something.

Addi scooted away from her, her eyebrows raised. 'Is there something you're not telling me, Lex Satchell?'

I nearly kissed our boss and, given half the chance, would do it, and more, again. But need like that scares me, because every bad decision Joelle made was born out of passion and rooted in her obsession over a man. But I liked it. I like him.

Lex shook her head and looked away. She was making a big deal about nothing. She wasn't even going to see Cole again. He'd hired a car, but he didn't like being driven around by a chauffeur, so driving him had been a one-time thing. It was a one-and-done situation. She should stop thinking about him and move on.

'What aren't you telling me, Lex?'

Lex remembered the fear on Addi's face earlier and tossed her sister's question back in her face. When Addi wrinkled her nose and looked away, Lex knew she'd hit a target she hadn't known existed. Anxiety washed over her, pushing ice into her veins. 'Addi, what aren't you telling me?'

Addi stood up and stretched, placing her fists on her slim hips and arching her back. 'I'm going in. It's freezing out here and I'm getting cold.'

Lex was about to push when her phone beeped with a loud notification. She frowned and opened the message from the unknown number.

I have a dinner engagement. Pick me up from the office in an hour fifteen. CT.

Her stomach rolled over and her knees melted, just a little, at the thought of seeing him again.

Oh, Lord, she was in so much trouble here.

CHAPTER FOUR

ON THE MOTORWAY, Lex hit a puddle, eased off the accelerator and flicked her windscreen wipers onto a higher setting. She darted a look at Cole, who sat in the passenger seat next to her, his expression as remote as the endless, empty Skeleton Coast. When he'd sent her the text message earlier telling her he required her services this evening, her heart had bounced around her chest and she'd wondered if, like her, he couldn't stop thinking about their almost kiss.

She mentally slapped herself. Cole was a guy in his mid-thirties, someone who'd probably had a few serious relationships, many affairs and more than a few one-night stands. He hadn't given their encounter any more thought than the brand of fuel she put in her car.

She might not have been able to think of anything else, but he was far more experienced and sophisticated than she could ever be.

Sitting next to him and wishing he'd kiss her again, hoping that he was seeing her as a woman, not an employee, was an exercise in sheer stupidity. 'Thank you for making yourself available,' Cole said. 'I know it was short notice.'

'It's my job and not a problem. Why did you change your mind about driving yourself?'

'I haven't,' Cole replied. 'I wasn't happy with the hire car my assistant organised and had it returned. Somehow, the message that I required a replacement car was lost along the way.'

Lex grimaced at the annoyance she heard in his voice. She was glad she hadn't been on the other side of the phone when Cole demanded to know why he didn't have a car at the end of the day. In casual clothes he was impressive and sexy but, dressed in a deep-grey suit and a patterned tie in metallic shades of copper and gold, he looked powerful and remote.

Yet she wasn't intimidated. And her attraction to him had nothing to do with the fact that he wore ten-thousand-dollar designer suits, sported an outrageously expensive wristwatch and splashed designer cologne on his face—she really wouldn't mind burying her nose in his neck and staying there—but everything to do with their very combustible chemistry.

She still, rather desperately, wanted to know how his mouth tasted and whether, when she was plastered against him, her body would stop missing his. How could she miss something she'd never experienced? She had no idea, but she did.

The Chauffeur's Inconvenient Attraction to the CEO... Her life could be the title of a romance novel.

'I was out of line earlier and I apologise.'

Lex grimaced and turned her head away.

Be cool…pretend it didn't mean anything. Do not let him know that you've thought of nothing more since leaving him yesterday.

'It wasn't…optimal,' she agreed. Optimal? Where had that word come from?

'I want to assure you it was an aberration.' *Wow.* And how was she supposed to take that statement? Was she an aberration? Was almost kissing his driver an aberration? Kissing at all?

She stopped at a traffic light, turned to face him and lifted her arched eyebrows. In the dim light of the inside of the car, she saw colour touch his cheeks.

'I never lose control like that,' he admitted, shoving his hand through his hair and looking genuinely confused. She thought about pointing out that nothing had happened, that they hadn't actually kissed, but honesty had her admitting that, had they not heard those voices in the hallway, they would've kissed. And, possibly, done more.

'Are you tired? Overworked? Stressed?' Lex asked him instead, interested, despite her irritation—an *aberration?*—in what made him tick.

'All of the above,' Cole replied, 'All the time. It's my default mode.'

His deep sigh filled the car. 'It's been a very long, tough six months.'

What did that mean and how did it relate to what had almost happened between them? Did he only kiss strangers when he was stressed?

'I apologise, Ms Satchell.'

The traffic light turned green and Lex pulled away.

They could discuss this to death, but she suspected she wouldn't get any satisfactory answers, so maybe it was better to put this behind them. Yes, she wanted him but that was her impetuosity talking, her long-neglected libido. It was time to be sensible and sober, to remember what was important—kissing him again wasn't, working as his driver was.

And this was the perfect opportunity to raise the subject. 'Cole—Mr Thorpe—I need to ask you whether I can get back to work as your driver.'

'I told you, I prefer to drive myself.'

Lex swallowed her growl. Fine, she got that he liked driving himself, but he didn't understand that his wanting to haul himself around Cape Town was making a serious dent in her income. She was paid a piddly retainer, but she earned the bulk of her money when she put in the kilometres behind the wheel. Driving Cole around would be an excellent way to bring cash to their communal table. And she wasn't too proud to tell him that. She needed money, and his being independent was blocking her from getting it. She wasn't asking for charity. She was asking him for the opportunity to do her job.

'Thorpe Industries only pays me a small retainer to be on call, but I only earn decent money when I drive. So your independence is affecting my earnings,' she said, keeping her tone as business-like as possible. He didn't need to know that the girls needed new winter pyjamas, that she needed to pay for next term's module and that her car desperately needed some work.

She felt his gaze on her face, but Lex kept her eyes

on the traffic, watching for any sudden moves by impatient truckers or taxi drivers. He did, of course, have the right to drive himself. Nothing in her contract with Thorpe Industries stated that the owner or employees were obliged to use her services. But, damn, she hoped he would because, A, his was a very nice face and body to drive around and, B, she hoped he was nice enough to put aside his needs, wants or preferences so that she, or anyone else, could earn a reasonable wage. It was just the decent thing to do…

'Pick me up from my hotel at seven tomorrow morning,' Cole told her, his voice gruff. 'When I get to the office, I can give you my schedule for the day, but I usually end quite late.'

Lex did a mental fist-pump as she turned down the road to where Snell's, the restaurant, was situated. Looking for parking, she was grateful Storm was on leave from her au pair job, as she could do the school run for the next week or so, and then it would be the winter holidays. Surely Cole would be gone by mid-July? Lex reversed the car into an empty parking bay—her parallel parking skills were on point tonight—and briefly closed her eyes. Cole was prepared to let her drive him so she didn't have to worry about her income for the next few weeks. *Yay.*

Now all she had to do was stop thinking about his big body, his mouth and how his hands would feel on her body, on her breasts, between her legs.

Lex pulled up to the blackened windows of the restaurant and peered through the darkness at the small gold plaque on the side of the closed door. Snell's. It was a good indication that you were a fine-dining restaurant when all you needed as advertising was a twelve-inch black square with gold writing.

'Thank you,' Lex told him when she switched the ignition off. She nodded at the restaurant. 'I hope you have a good meal.'

He looked at her, his expression a little annoyed. 'What will you do while you are waiting for me?' he enquired.

In the boot was a bag containing her laptop and her study notes. She'd noticed an all-night café attached to a brightly lit garage on her way in and she'd thought she'd wait there and study until Cole was ready to be picked up. But she was just a car door down from the restaurant entrance and there were security guards outside and at each end of the brightly lit street. She would be perfectly safe waiting for him right there.

'I'm going to stay here and, when you're done, I'm going to drive you back to your hotel.'

Because that was her job for now. It wasn't for ever. In two years she'd have her degree and would look for work in her field. Time flew by quickly and, one day, working as a chauffeur—and as a maid and as a coffee barista…she'd done both—would be a distant memory.

'One of the reasons I hate having a chauffeur is that I loathe knowing people are waiting around for me,' Cole muttered. He undid his seat belt and Lex reached for her door handle, about to hop out and run around the car to open the door for him. His hand on her arm stopped her progress and she felt an electrical buzz skitter up her arm. 'I've agreed to you driving me, but if you open one door for me I will fire you.'

Her lips twitched, amused and surprised by his lack of snobbery. She tipped her head to the side, knowing this was a battle she wouldn't win. 'I'm going to get out of the car and get a laptop bag from the boot,' she told him. She lifted her hands in mock surrender. 'I promise I won't come anywhere near your door.'

'Smarty pants,' Cole muttered. 'Stay there.'

Since the heavens were dripping again—this time it was a fine, persistent drizzle—Lex opted to wait in her warm seat, and within a minute Cole opened her door and dumped her laptop bag in her lap. 'Will you be okay?' he asked. Lex swallowed at the concern in his voice. When had someone, outside of her sisters, last wondered whether she'd be alright? She couldn't actually remember.

She nodded, conscious that the rain was darkening his grey suit to black and dampening the waves in his hair. 'Cole—sorry, Mr Thorpe—I'll be fine. Go inside, *please*.'

He narrowed his eyes at her and poked his index finger into her thigh. 'Calling me anything but Cole would be another fireable offence.'

All righty, then. Cole slammed her door shut and walked over to the black door, and the security guard whipped it open for him. But, instead of walking inside, he reached for his wallet and pulled out what looked to be a high-denomination note. He nodded at the car, then at her, and when Lex saw the bouncer nodding in agreement as he took Cole's money she knew she had her own private security guard.

Sweet, she thought. And thoughtful. Two things she hadn't expected Cole Thorpe to be.

'Snell's was voted as the world's fiftieth best restaurant in 2021,' Jude said, sitting opposite him.

It was good to be with Jude, Cole decided as he looked around the restaurant, taking in the surprisingly warm industrial space with a busy, open kitchen in the middle of the long restaurant. They'd attended university together in London and Jude had gone on to inherit the Cape Town based Fisher Holdings, a well-respected hospitality and leisure empire.

Cole looked up at the cloud of steel discs hanging from the ceiling, and idly wondered how many of the world's best restaurants he'd eaten at over the past ten years. Twenty? Thirty? More?

He'd eaten sushi made by the master Jiro Ono at Sukiyabashi Jiro, eaten duck at Noma, Copenhagen, and Massimo Bottura's 'Five Ages of Parmigiano Reggiano' at his restaurant in Modena.

But the worst of it was that he knew, without thought or hesitation, that no meal he'd ever eaten would hold the complexity of Lex's mouth. She would be, as the French said, *bonne bouche*, a delicious mouthful. He wanted, more than anything else, to feast on her.

He understood sexual attraction—at thirty-six, he should—but he couldn't work out how she'd slipped under his skin with such ease. She'd invaded his thoughts and, because he couldn't stop thinking about her, he felt a little panicky and angsty. And annoyed.

He didn't have time for distractions, damn it. Why here? Why now? Was his reaction to her a consequence of the stress he'd been under lately and the denial of his revenge against his father? Were his emotions, frustration and disappointment, leaking out of the steel vault he'd locked them into and masquerading as need and interest? It had been such a weird time lately that anything was possible.

Not recognising himself, frustrated by his strange thoughts—he never gave any woman this much space in his head, ever—he tossed back his whisky. When he opened his eyes, he saw Jude looking from his glass to his face and back to his glass again. 'Tough few days?' he asked.

Cole dug his thumb and index finger into his eye sockets, rubbed hard and shook his head. 'No more than usual,' he lied. He'd only nearly kissed—ravished—his chauffeur an hour after he'd met her. And, despite never having employed a driver, he now had one.

Jude called the waiter over, ordered the tasting menu and leaned back in his chair, his eyes on Cole's face. They'd become friendly while playing for the same university based social rugby team seventeen years ago and somehow, despite their insane schedules, had remained friends. As students, they'd taken a skiing holiday every January and they'd kept up the tradition, carving out time to do something they both loved. When they'd been young, they'd saved hard to spend a week on the slopes. These days, they still stayed out all day, alternating between snowboarding and black diamond runs, but instead of returning to a youth hostel they enjoyed private suites and had immediate access to steam rooms and experienced masseurs to work out the kinks seventeen years had put into their muscles.

'Did you ever get hold of your brother?' Jude asked.

Cole shook his head. 'No, and I've been told not to expect him to make contact. As I've recently discovered, he's been practising Buddhism for years and often expressed a wish to join a monastery. Nobody took him seriously until he did.'

Jude leaned back in his seat, his narrowed gaze penetrating. 'Are you very sure you want to get rid of the Thorpe assets, Cole? You are dismantling your family's century-old business.'

His family—the one he'd never been allowed to be a part of? His first memories were of being confused about why his father wouldn't pay him any attention, why he only ever focused on Sam. His parents had divorced when he'd been four, and he'd spent his childhood wondering what was wrong with him, and why Sam had got to spend time with their mum while he'd never seen his father.

He'd frequently asked his mum for an explanation and had been told that his father was 'funny that way', and that once his mind was made up nothing would change it. When he'd mentally divorced himself from his father, he'd vowed he'd make a fortune to rival that of his father's, and that he'd do it for himself, by himself. But he'd still craved their attention. What better way to get that than by taking control of their empire?

Taking away Thorpe Industries had been the only way he could think of to make them notice him but they'd both dodged that bullet.

Damn them.

Cole picked up the menu and scanned it, frustrated. Up until his father died, he'd had a plan, a reason to work long hours, to push himself. He'd wanted to be in a position where his father and brother couldn't ignore him, where they'd have to look at him across a conference table and know that he held all the power, their financial lives in his hands. They would've been forced to acknowledge him, deal with him and respect him.

But, by dying and stepping aside, they'd both robbed him of that opportunity and him of his purpose. He felt like a leaf on a river in a flood, swept away and out of control, aimless.

'So, I've been looking through your South African-based assets,' Jude told him. 'I'll buy all your hospitality interests, except the ski-lodge.'

'Why don't you want the ski-lodge?' Cole asked. The waiter had picked up two plates from the pass and he hoped they were destined for their table. He was famished.

'Firstly, it's a ski-lodge in Africa, dude. Yeah, it's in the mountains, very remote, and the area gets snow in winter, but it's never guaranteed.'

'Surely they have snow machines?' Cole suggested, leaning back so that the waiter could deposit his plate in front of him.

'They have them. Look, judging by the photographs, it's a stunning place. Your father spent a king's ransom renovating it. But to recoup those costs, your hospitality division had to stratospherically hike the accommodation costs. South Africans who can afford to pay those rates can afford to fly to Gstaad or Aspen, Whistler or Verbier, where there are numerous runs, guaranteed snow and world-class facilities,' Jude explained. 'Frankly, I don't understand the decision-making behind the ski resort at all but I've heard it was your father's pet project.'

Cole frowned. Why, when he had businesses around the world, would Grenville have cared so much about a ten-bedroom boutique hotel in a remote part of South Africa?

And why, if he didn't care about his father, Thorpe assets or the family empire, did that puzzle arouse his interest and curiosity?

It was eleven-thirty when Cole tapped on the driver's window of the company SUV. Lex turned her head and looked at him through the rain-splattered glass, and it took her a while to switch from whatever she'd been reading to her job as his driver. She hit the lock to open the passenger door and Cole ducked around the hood of the vehicle, clutching his fancy takeout box. It was raining harder now, and he felt icy drops hit his hair and roll down the back of his neck. Africa was supposed to be about sunshine, but all he'd experienced was wild and wet weather, and more was on the way.

Fabulous.

He climbed into the passenger seat and balanced the box on the dashboard, shoving his hands into his hair to dispel the rain drops. Without asking, Lex punched the button to start the car and warm air hit his face and chest. 'Thanks.'

'How was dinner?' she asked as she closed her textbook. He looked down to see that it was a battered copy, something to do with the evolution of neuro-science. An array of sticky notes poked out from its pages and Lex slipped the book and her equally old laptop into her bag. Zipping it up, she placed the bag behind his seat. She'd pulled her long hair back into a messy bun, and he reached across and removed a pen from behind her ear and handed it to her.

'Thanks,' she replied, blushing. She tossed it into the console and pulled on her seatbelt.

He saw her glance at the box before looking away.

'Back to the hotel?' she asked.

'In a minute,' He reached for the box, flipped open the lid and handed it to her. Lex took it with a puzzled frown, looking down.

'What is this?'

'You picked me up at six, which means you prob-ably haven't eaten,' Cole explained. He reached into his jacket pocket and brought out a set of chopsticks, which he handed to her. 'Peter Snell boxed it up for me—it's a selection from his tasting menu.'

Lex's mouth dropped open and it took all of Cole's

determination not to bend down and cover that luscious mouth with his. 'He's a Michelin-starred chef,' she stated.

'So?'

'You asked a Michelin-starred chef for a take-away?' Lex asked, stupefied. 'For me?'

What was the big deal? He'd asked, Snell had said yes, here he was.

Cole waved the chopsticks in the air. 'Do you want these or not?' he asked, hiding his smile when Lex snatched them out of his hand. She slid them between her fingers and lifted a piece of pastry-wrapped fish to her mouth.

'It's tuna, obviously. But what's between the fish and the pastry? It tastes citrusy but I can't identify it.'

'Yuzu and enoki mushrooms, I think.' He pointed to the other dishes. 'Veal, Jerusalem artichokes, scallops and some orange-chocolate-chilli thing.'

'Oh, yum.' Lex took the second bite of tuna before darting a horrified look at him. 'Sorry, I can eat this later. Let me get you back to the hotel.'

'Eat, Lex. I'm not in a hurry. All that waits for me at the hotel is more work.'

Lex waved her chopsticks in the air. 'You're going back to the hotel to work? It's after eleven.'

He pushed his chair back and stretched out his legs. He linked his hands across his flat stomach and rolled his head around. 'Says the woman who was working up until ten minutes ago.'

'Mmm, that's because I have an assignment due.'

She opened the lid to the artichoke dish and stared down. 'I've never eaten artichokes before.'

'They are delicious,' Cole assured her and watched as she took a cautious bite. She'd surprised him tonight, in so many ways. She'd been so up and honest about needing work, so unembarrassed about telling him that she needed to drive to earn money. He admired her put-it-out-there attitude. She didn't seem to care what he, or anyone else, thought about her.

When he'd told her that he didn't need her to drive him, he hadn't given a thought to how his arbitrary decision might affect her. He did what he liked, what suited him, and hadn't given her needs a second thought. He felt ashamed of himself, annoyed by his self-serving attitude.

He had to do better, be better. Think more about people and how his actions affected them.

Though maybe a part of him not wanting Lex to drive him was because he knew that in the confines of a car, surrounded by her smell, hearing her rich voice, he'd be constantly distracted by what he wanted to do to her in bed—or on a desk, or up against a wall. He didn't like being distracted or frustrated—who did? He'd thought it better to put her, and his fantasies, out of sight and mind.

Hah! No chance of that now. 'What are you studying?' he asked.

'Psychology—specifically forensic psychology,' she told him, her attention on her food. She'd already demolished half of the food and didn't look like she was going to stop any time soon. He didn't mind.

All that waited for him was spreadsheets and emails, and boring ones at that. He'd much rather sit in a stationary car in the rain with Lex than be alone in his hotel room.

And that was strange because, after an evening spent in a busy restaurant, even if he did eat with someone he knew well, he normally couldn't wait for the quiet of his hotel room.

'Why psychology?' he asked, intrigued by her. It was obvious that she was intelligent, but she worked as a driver and she needed flexible work hours. Where were her parents, and why was she raising her sisters? Was that why she hadn't finished her degree years ago?

Lex inspected the perfectly round medallion of veal. She grimaced and raised her eyes to look at him. 'Veal is baby cow, right?'

He smiled at her squeamishness. 'Think of it as coming in a polystyrene tray wrapped in plastic,' he told her. 'And, trust me, you want to taste that, it's the best dish on the menu.'

'Good enough for me.' Without hesitation, Lex popped the veal into her mouth. She chewed, tipped her head to the side and incredulity crossed her face. He wondered if the same look of wonder and contentment would cross her face when she orgasmed. He thought it would, but at double the intensity. And he was desperate to see her do exactly that.

'So, psychology?' he prompted, dragging his thoughts off his vivid imaginings of Lex's long, pale body, her hair bright against the white sheets of his bed. He felt his trousers getting smaller and counted to ten. Then to twenty.

He. Paid. Her. Salary.

Nope, the sexy image wouldn't be dispelled.

Holy Batman.

'Oh…right.' She stared out of the window again, as if she was trying to find the right words. 'Initially, I studied it because I wanted to try to work out why certain people in my life acted the way they acted, did what they did. Then I realised it would take me a lifetime to understand if there was any sense to be made, so I switched to forensic because the criminal mind fascinates me.'

'So, no criminals in your family?' he asked, joking.

'Not that I know of,' Lex replied. 'Criminally stupid, sure. Actual miscreants? I don't think so.' She looked down at her supper and blew out her cheeks. 'I am so full.'

She only had the orange-chocolate-chilli tart left to eat. And, if she didn't, he would. It was the perfect end to the meal. 'You've got to try it,' he told her. 'It's stunning.'

She looked at him, placed her hand on her stomach and popped the bite-sized confection into her mouth. She chewed, looked up at the ceiling and chewed some more, looking undecided and underwhelmed as she did so. Oh, come on! How could she not like it? It was delicious.

'Well?' he demanded when she swallowed and put her chopsticks into the box and closed the lid.

She took the handkerchief he pulled from the inside pocket of his jacket and delicately wiped her mouth, then her fingers, on the cool cotton.

'Not terrible,' she told him, and it took him a few beats for him to realise that her tongue was firmly in her cheek and she was teasing him.

He put his hand on the back of her neck and shook her very gently. He couldn't keep his lips from inching upwards into a smile. 'That's probably the best dessert you've ever eaten.'

As soon as the words left his mouth, he realised that he sounded as if he was putting her down, highlighting the financial differences between them. He hadn't meant to. It had been one of the best meals of his life too.

'Absolutely,' Lex replied, shrugging. 'There's no question that it's the best meal I've ever eaten. Thank you for arranging that for me.'

He'd lost track of all the exceptional meals he'd eaten in his life, but watching Lex eat bits and pieces from Patrick Snell's tasting menu from a box in a car in Cape Town was his best food experience this decade. Possibly ever.

Damn it. He was in a world of trouble here. And his honest, direct driver had put him there.

Brilliant.

'Let's get you back to the Vane,' Lex said, starting the car.

And, when they got there, it took all his willpower to leave the car without asking her to join him upstairs.

CHAPTER FIVE

COLE WAS EXHAUSTED, thanks to lying awake in his hotel room and fantasising about his heavily freckled, red-headed driver. He'd spent the past week reading too many profit and loss statements and balance sheets and his brain was fried. He'd been working twenty-four-seven for months now, and he knew himself well enough to know that he needed a break, to step back and away for a day, maybe two.

A weekend of doing nothing more intellectually stimulating than breathing would be the best way for him to rest and recharge. Yesterday, Lex had asked him if she could have the morning off and he'd agreed, taking the keys to the company vehicle from her hand. He pulled the SUV into its designated parking space in the underground garage and sighed. The car smelled like Lex, and he was once again bombarded by the image of her red hair, recalling the passion in her green eyes as he'd lowered his head to kiss her. He could almost feel her elegant hands in his hair, the feel of her long legs around his hips.

Why couldn't he get the memory of that kiss-that-never-happened out of his mind?

He definitely needed a break. Or a lobotomy.

Cole grabbed his laptop bag, exited his car and slammed the door shut, mentally running through his schedule. He had virtual meetings all morning but he was free from lunch onwards. He was planning to leave the city for the weekend and had asked his assistant to book two nights at one of the upmarket safari operations in the area. He knew there were a couple just a few hours' drive from Cape Town.

Could he ask Lex to drive him and take her along? Would that work, was that even an option?

No, of course it wasn't, for all the reasons he'd previously thought of and, possibly, a hundred he hadn't considered.

Cole felt an icy wind swirl around his neck and heard the unmistakable sound of a car with a hole in its exhaust. He turned and watched a yellow hatchback roll up the ramp. Through a windscreen sporting a crack in the top right-hand corner, he caught a glimpse of red hair and a pale face behind the wheel. A cool blonde sat next to Lex, and another blonde and two little girls, one with hair as red as Lex's, sat in the back.

Were these her sisters? *All* of them?

Standing next to the lift, partially hidden by a concrete column, Cole winced at the sound of squeaking brakes—her brake pads needed replacing—and he watched the older blonde, dressed in a black power suit, exit the car. Lex switched off the engine and the little girls left the car, taking turns to hug the first blonde. Lex stood between her door and the frame, looking at them over the rusty roof.

'Bye, Addi,' they said. Right, so the blonde was Addison Fields, and she worked in his hospitality and leisure division.

'I might as well drive Storm and the girls straight from here to the airport, Addi,' Lex said as Addison hugged the second blonde, whom he assumed was Storm. 'It's a bit early but there's no point in going home first and leaving again in fifteen minutes.'

'We're going to the beach, we're going to the beach,' the little redhead chanted, spinning around in circles. Cole shivered, unable to understand her excitement. It was wet, windy and cold, weather that only Arctic penguins enjoyed.

Storm chivvied the small girls back into the car and the three women stood in a circle, their voices carrying over to him.

Lex, who faced him, smiled and it was like a fist ploughed into his sternum. Her joyous, wide grin could power a small city. 'Five years, guys. It's been five years since I've had a break. Am I mean to be this excited?' She bit her lower lip, suddenly looking deflated.

Storm rubbed her arm and Addison shook her head before speaking. 'No, babe. You know you're the best sister ever and you've been with them constantly since the day they arrived. I go to work and don't spend a lot of time with them. You do. Take these three weeks and enjoy them, Lex, because, honey, you deserve it.'

Cole recalled his mother telling him that children were expensive, time-consuming and limited your freedom.

His mother, so warm and affectionate.

'What are you going to do with all your spare time, Lex?' Storm asked her.

Have an affair with him? Cole wished.

'I'd love to take a road trip and just drive and drive and drive, but I have to ferry Cole Thorpe around. The money is too good for me to take a holiday right now. Besides, my car is shot, and fuel prices are crazy. So, in between driving him, I'll just nap, study and binge-watch box sets.'

'Maybe we could take a day trip up to Lamberts Bay,' Addison suggested.

Lex smiled. 'I'd love that,' she answered, but Cole knew that wasn't what she wanted or needed. She wanted the open road, the freedom of driving. It wasn't about the destination but the journey: the sound of tyres on the tarmac, the growl of an engine, the silence and vastness of an uninhabited landscape.

'I'm sorry about booking my car in for a service today. If I knew that the girls were flying to Durban today, I would've scheduled it for another time.'

Lex shrugged. 'Their holiday was a last-minute arrangement, how were you to know?'

Addison sent a doubtful look at the yellow car. 'But I hate you doing long trips in your car, Lex, or being on the highway.'

Lex wrinkled her nose. 'I know, I do too, especially in this weather. The tyres are smoother than I'd like.' She hesitated before speaking again. 'I know it's expensive, but I think we should put them in a cab.'

Cole cranked his head to look at her tyres and noticed that they definitely needed replacing. In wet weather, they would slide all over the road.

'I'll pay for it,' Storm offered.

Addison shook her head. 'Honey, you paid for the flights to Durban, and you're going to be entertaining the girls for the next three weeks. You need to save your money. I think the house credit card has a little room on it, Lex.'

Lex nodded. 'Okay, cool. Let me just park and I'll order one.'

This was ridiculous. There was a perfectly good SUV sitting right there, with a full tank of fuel, doing nothing. He saw Lex's eyes widen as he stepped out from behind the pillar and her gorgeous mouth dropped open.

'Good morning, Lex,' he said, deliberately formal.

Her face pinkened under her freckles. 'Uh…morning.' He walked up to Addison, holding out his hand. 'I presume you are Addison Fields? I'm Cole Thorpe.'

Addison looked a little dazed but she put her hand in his. 'I'm sorry we haven't connected personally before now, Mr Thorpe.'

'I hear Jude Fisher has been running you ragged,' he replied. He looked down at the two little girls who were looking at him with wide eyes through the back window.

'Sisters?' he asked, aiming his question at Lex.

'Yep. This is my middle sister, Storm, and Nixi and Snow are in the car,' she told him.

Cole looked down at the little girls, who couldn't have been more different in looks if they'd tried. The older was a dark-haired, dark-eyed beauty while the younger had Lex's red hair, complexion and eye colour. This was what Lex's little girl would look like, he realised—all long limbs, pale skin, red hair and freckles.

Addison bit her lip, looking embarrassed. 'I know I'm late, Mr Thorpe, but I'll be up in a minute. I just need to sort something out.'

In other words: *shoo*. But nobody told him where to go or what to do. He looked at Lex and nodded to the SUV. 'There's no need to order a cab.'

Lex's eyebrows raised in silent disapproval of his eavesdropping. He shrugged. 'Voices travel in empty spaces. Use the company car to take your family to the airport, Lex. The roads are slick and it's the safest option in the rain.'

Lex lifted her nose in the air and her mouth thinned. He knew that she was about to refuse but Addison beat her to the punch. 'Thank you so much, Mr Thorpe, that's incredibly generous of you. We'll contribute to the cost of the fuel.'

He appreciated the offer. 'That's not necessary, Addison. I am aware of how hard you've been working lately, and I'm happy to help.'

Still looking at Addison, he asked her whether she was free to meet with him shortly. 'I've been meaning to catch up with you and chat about your future with Thorpe Industries.'

He saw the flash of fear in her eyes and immediately looked at Lex and saw the same scared expression on her lovely face. Storm just bent her head and looked at the grubby floor. The realisation that the three women were terrified Addison was going to lose her job hit him with all the force of a sledgehammer, and he was reminded that his actions had real-life, real-world consequences.

Judging by the fact that they were debating whether to hire a cab or not, money was very tight.

'Half an hour?' he asked Addison before looking at Lex and handing her the keys to the SUV.

'Drive safely, Lex. It's horrible out there,' he told her, sounding serious.

'Yes, I know.' She nodded, swallowed and nodded again. 'Thank you. I appreciate you letting me use the car.'

She didn't like him knowing they were in a jam but wasn't too proud to express her gratitude. He was already deeply attracted to this woman. He didn't need to like her as well.

He heard the lift open behind him and nodded. 'Have a good trip, ladies. Addison, I'll see you in half an hour. Lex, I'd like to see you when you get back too.'

'Me?' Lex responded, confused. 'Why?'

He couldn't tell her that he needed to know that she was back safely, that he needed to see her face, so instead of answering he stepped into the lift and hit the side of his fist against the button to close the lift doors.

He glanced at his watch as the lift took him to his penthouse office. He didn't have any trips scheduled for today, and after hearing that Lex needed some time off last night he'd given her the rest of the weekend off, telling her he wouldn't need her again until Monday morning.

Right, he had a couple of hours to work out a reason for wanting to see her again. He was a smart guy. He was sure he could find something to tell her that she would believe.

Because telling her that he wanted to know that she was safe and that he'd missed seeing her face this morning, that he wanted to kiss her again—that he wanted to spend the weekend with her, preferably in bed—was out of the question. It was a shock to realise that, even if sex was off the table, he wouldn't mind her company, seeing her blinding white smile, exploring her bright mind.

What? Was he catching feelings for this woman? Was that the strange sensation he was experiencing? If he was, he'd better stop. And he could. He could gather up his emotions and shove them behind the sky-high wall he'd built. He'd done it often enough before and could, and would, do it again.

After meeting with Addison—and reassuring her that he'd talk to Jude about him taking her on when he acquired his hospitality portfolio—Cole had a pounding headache and a craving for a decent cup of coffee.

The only down side of having a virtual assistant was that he had to track down and make his own coffee.

On crazily busy mornings like this one, not having coffee delivered was a pain in his butt.

Cole leaned back in his leather seat and looked out of his window onto a spectacular view of Lion's Head. Or, it would be spectacular, if the famous landmark wasn't obscured by driving rain. A cold front had moved in and another, bigger one was on its way.

He wasn't going to see the African sun for a while.

He thought back to his meeting with Addison. Shortly after sitting down opposite him, Addison had expressed her sympathy for his dad's passing and told him Grenville had hired her a few months after she'd finished her degree, a wet-behind-the-ears kid with no experience, and had become her mentor.

His father had taken a chance on Addison, a stranger, but hadn't given him the time of day. It shouldn't still hurt but it did. Addison wasn't the first person Grenville had looked after and mentored—there was a young woman in India, and a few people in the States, who hadn't stopped singing his praises.

Grenville had been able to see the potential in other people but had never offered his youngest son what he so readily gave to others. Did Grenville know that he'd graduated from the London School of Economics with a brilliant degree, that he'd got his MBA in record time? That he was the youngest hedge fund manager employed at Hershel and Grimm, one of the oldest, most respected investment firms in the world? Did he know he'd left them after a year and had taken most of their clients—their choice, not his—with him? That he had been a millionaire by thirty, a billionaire a few years later? Grenville had evidently cared far more for other people than he did for his own son.

It was that simple.

Why? What had he done? It was painful not to know. But being ostracised had made him tough, made him resilient, and, damn, it had made him determined to show his brother and father what he could do, what he'd achieved. Had his father lived, they would've been forced to acknowledge his achievement, to accept that he'd far exceeded the low bar that had been set for him. That he was their equal in every way that counted.

He felt cheated, like a child who'd reached for his stack of presents on Christmas day to have them whipped away and replaced with a chunk of coal. He'd so badly wanted his father's approval, a hint of respect, because if he couldn't have his love—and that had never been on the cards—he'd have settled for respect and approval. Love: it was such a stupid emotion. He'd been right to walk away from it, to stop looking for it. It caused nothing but heartache. It was far easier to live his life emotionally unconnected.

His eyes fell onto the Rossdale Ski Lodge folder, and he picked it up and banged its corner on his desk. He felt jumpy and irritated, and unable to focus.

Unfortunately, his inability to concentrate wasn't something new.

Since his dad's death and Sam's disappearance, it

felt as if all he'd done was react. He was a guy who called the shots, he didn't take them.

Right, focus, Thorpe.

What was he going to do about Rossdale Ski Lodge, the asset Jude didn't want, and the acquisition and the refurbishment of which puzzled both Jude and Addison?

He understood why. The cost of the renovation and refurbishment had meant that they'd had to charge exorbitantly outrageous nightly rates, and the lodge had had just a handful of customers in the eighteen months it had been open. It was run by a couple who were paid a huge salary to do nothing.

He needed to see the place for himself, to try and figure out what his father had been thinking when he'd purchased the property. He wouldn't get that information from balance sheets and spreadsheets so that meant a trip to the far-away property. Cole pulled up a map and grimaced when he saw that it was more than a twelve-hour drive to reach the lodge.

It would be quicker to hire a private plane, then a helicopter. That was likely how his father had tackled the journey.

Cole reached for his phone, thinking there had to be someone in this place who could get him a cup of coffee. He was about to call down to Reception when he heard knocking and a bright head appeared between the door and its frame.

His heart settled and sighed, and he waved Lex to come inside. When he saw that she carried two mega cups of coffee and a brown grease-stained bag, he nearly wept with joy and briefly considered proposing to her.

The thought made him smile and, funnily enough, didn't make his skittish heart want to bolt for the hills. *Weird.*

Cole had to stop himself from lunging across the desk to take the cup she held out. He lifted the mug to his mouth and took a hit of the hot, rich liquid. It was black and strong, just the way he liked it.

Lex took the seat opposite him, amusement turning her eyes lighter. 'Wow. A little addicted, are we?'

'A lot addicted,' Cole replied. 'Thank you, you have no idea how much I needed this.'

'I'm beginning to get the idea. You wanted to see me, I wanted coffee, so I picked up one for you as well.'

He couldn't remember when someone had last brought him a cup of coffee, or anything else, just because it occurred to them. It was a small gesture, but to Cole it felt as if someone had handed him a winning lottery ticket.

Cole nodded to the paper bag. 'And that?'

Lex smiled. 'That is a thank you gift for letting me use the SUV. I know this tiny bakery, and they do a limited run of the most fabulous chocolate croissants in the city. I called the owner and begged her to keep two for me. You loved the dessert from the other night, so I thought you'd enjoy this too.'

Cole reached for the bag, opened it and closed his eyes as the delicious smell of butter, chocolate and pastry hit his nostrils. He'd run eight miles on the treadmill and done a weightlifting session in the hotel gym this morning and eaten only bran and yoghurt for breakfast. He deserved something sweet and artery-clogging.

He broke off a piece of the croissant and nodded in approval when she did the same. He popped it into his mouth and closed his eyes at the hit of sweetness and spice.

As he ate, he tried to keep himself from launching across the table to find out what the combination of Lex and croissants tasted like. He watched as she unwound her scarf and shed her battered but still chic bomber-style leather jacket. Today's tight long-sleeved T-shirt was a pretty mint colour and her skinny jeans disappeared into knee-high boots.

'Did your sisters get off okay?' he asked.

'Yes. Snow cried a little, but she was fine by the time I left.'

Cole stood up, walked around the desk and perched on the edge of it, facing Lex, his thigh just an inch or two from her knee. Giving into temptation, he stroked the pad of his thumb across her cheekbone. 'Why do your younger sisters live with you, Lex? Where's their mother?'

Those incredible eyes met his and he saw a flicker of pain cross her face. 'In Thailand. She's been there since we were teenagers. We've had them for five years,' Lex answered him, and he didn't hear a hint of rancour or resentment in her voice. 'Nixi was three, Snow two.'

So she'd been their mother, father and sister and

the pillars of their world for five years and would be for the rest of their lives. She would've been twenty-three or twenty-four when they'd dropped into her life. He rubbed the back of his neck, unable to understand how nonchalant she sounded, as though taking in two small children was what young adults did every day.

'And your father? Their father? Or fathers?' he demanded, unable to make sense of the dynamic.

Lex lifted one shoulder and he suspected her blasé expression was well-practised. 'My mum has a very relaxed attitude towards sex, and obviously contraception. And her lovers' names.'

Lex hesitated before continuing. 'She put the name of Addi's father on her birth certificate, and she married Storm's dad. My father was a guy called Seamus, but she's not completely sure if she got the right guy on the right night.'

'I don't get it. Weren't you angry? Frustrated? Bitter?'

'At what? Not knowing who my dad is or being left to raise the girls?'

'Either,' Cole replied. 'Both.'

'I can't be mad at my biological father. He doesn't know about me and never will. I was the result of a random hook-up between two very drunk, possibly high, people.' Lex shrugged and picked at a tiny thread on the cuff of her shirt. 'As for raising my half-sisters, how would being angry help? Nixi and Snow were already feeling lost and uprooted, they didn't need to know that they were unwanted too.'

His family hadn't given him a fraction of the love and care Lex—and the other sisters—showed those two little girls. They'd had all the money in the world but had been emotionally bankrupt. The sisters, from what he gathered, were short on cash but long on loyalty. He couldn't form the words to tell her how he was overwhelmingly impressed by her, that he admired her courage and intensely respected her, but she might get the message if he kissed her. So he did.

Lex sighed and her breath hit his lips, holding a hint of coffee, croissant and mint mouthwash. Cole fought the urge to take the kiss deeper, to haul her up so that her body was flush against his, her head tipped to take his deep, long and sexy kiss. Lex's fingers came up to rest on his jaw, rough with stubble. Her lips softened, he tasted her sigh and then her tongue came out to brush against his, spicy and delightful.

Her mouth was a revelation with soft, unpainted lips, as smooth and soft as expensive ice-cream. All he could think of was getting closer to her, to having his hands on that soft skin. Forgetting where he was, who he was, he stood up, pulled her to her feet and pushed her so that her back was to the wall next to his desk. He crowded her with his body, chest to chest, his knee between her thighs. He gripped her hips, enjoying her slim but curvy body, but he needed to know whether her skin was as soft as he imagined. He pulled her shirt from his jeans and slid his hand under her fabric, sighing at the silkiness of her skin. Lex wound her arms around his neck and kissed him, as hot for him as he was for her.

Cole felt his erection straining the fabric of his trousers, hot, heavy and desperate. He placed his hands on Lex's hips, easily lifting her so that their mouths were level. In a move that was as natural as it was unexpected, she wrapped her legs around his legs and rocked against him, releasing soft little sounds in the back of her throat.

Lex's elegant hands slipped under his shirt and he shuddered as her fingers danced up and down his spine, and dipped behind the waistband of his trousers. Needing to know more of her, to know everything, he placed his hand on her breast and drew his thumb across her nipple. Would it be as pink as her lips? Would she like it if he captured it between his tongue and the roof of his mouth…?

Damn, he needed a bed, but there was a desk just a foot or two from them…

There was a desk…and they were in his office and, because he didn't have a gatekeeper sitting at the secretary's desk next door, they could be interrupted at any second. And the last thing he wanted was interruptions.

So he pulled back, blew out a long stream of air and led her back to her chair, which she sank into with a long sigh. Cole reached for his coffee, resumed his previous position facing her and stretched out his legs.

'Another aberration, Cole?' she asked, looking him dead in the eye, and Cole felt pinned down. Damn, she was so direct.

'I don't understand.'

'You called our almost-kiss at the hotel an aberration,' Lex explained.

That hadn't been a good choice of words. Cole pushed his hand through his hair. 'No, but kissing you was…is…ill-advised. I'm your *boss*, Lex. I'm never anything but professional and the fact that you can make me lose my head is baffling.'

'If it's any consolation, I can't afford to put my job on the line by making out with my employer,' Lex told him. 'If you do sell your Cape Town assets, both Addi and I will lose our jobs, so I need to make bank while we can.'

While he had more money than most—a *lot* more money than most—he did understand the pressure of only having himself to rely on, of knowing that if he didn't make it work, nobody would do it for him. He couldn't promise Lex a flexible job, but he could reassure her about Addi. 'As I told Addison earlier, if I sell the hospitality sector to Jude Fisher I'll make Addison's job a condition of that sale. She won't have to accept Jude's offer, but he'll have to employ her for at least a year if he wants to buy my assets.'

She looked at him as if he'd hung the moon and stars. Damn it, he could get used to seeing that expression on her face. 'Thank you, Cole. That's… Wow, an incredible offer.'

It was and now he had to sell it to Jude. But, if he'd read his friend's expression correctly whenever Addison was mentioned, it wouldn't be a difficult negotiation.

He just wished he could do something for Lex. He

could write her a cheque but knew she'd never, in a million years, accept his charity. No, she needed to drive to earn money, and a germ of an idea started to percolate and bubble. If she drove him to Rhodes, where his ski-lodge was situated, she would earn a packet, far more than she usually would. And he'd be able to give her that road trip she seemed to want so much.

Cole stood up, his mind running a million miles a minute. He'd been planning to fly into Rhodes, in and out, but he could spare a few days out of his crazy schedule. He'd been running fast and hard for months, and a road trip would be as good for him as it would be for her. He felt a tingle on the back of his neck, a warm heat invading his veins. Was that excitement he felt? It had been so long, he didn't recognise it any more.

Lex looked down at his half-eaten croissant and he saw the longing on her face. He pushed the packet in her direction. 'Help yourself.'

'I shouldn't, I had a slice of pizza at the airport, but I will,' she replied, ripping off a piece and putting it into her mouth. Even when eating she was sexy.

Taking his seat again, he placed his elbows on the desk and looked at her. 'I need to get to Rhodes in the Eastern Cape. I'd need two days to get there, right?'

To her credit, Lex didn't blink at his change of subject. Neither did she demand to know why he'd kissed her or feel the need to analyse their encounter. 'Yeah. It's too long a drive to do it in one stretch. I mean, you could, but it would be crazy long.'

'Where would I stay the first night?'

'Colesberg, I guess.' Lex looked puzzled. 'But why drive if you can fly? It's so much quicker.'

'I'm not crazy about small planes or helicopters,' he lied. And it was a whopper. He adored anything with an engine and, one day, he intended to get his helicopter licence. But if he flew into Rhodes to see the ski-lodge he wouldn't have the excuse to take Lex along for the ride.

Cole asked himself what he was doing, what on earth was he thinking? Was he really going to take four, five days out of his schedule to drive to this ski-lodge so that he could give this emerald-eyed, tired, sometimes sad, sometimes feisty woman the road trip she so wanted? But suddenly he couldn't think of anything more he wanted to do.

Yes, he wanted to give her the break she needed, the road trip she'd said she wanted, to take her away from Cape Town and the demands of her busy life. It wasn't a Mediterranean beach holiday, but she would be getting away, doing something different. It was shocking to realise how much he wanted to whisk her away from real life.

But long hours in the car, being in close proximity, would either ratchet up their attraction or make them want to kill each other. If the latter happened, and he knew it wouldn't, he had the means to hire a helicopter to fly them back to Cape Town.

But what if they landed up in bed? The chances of that happening were sky-high because she was as physically attracted to him as he was to her. They were dry kindling meeting a spark…and with one kiss they could set Table Mountain on fire. But sex was sex, work was work, and he'd never let his personal feelings colour his views, so Lex's job would never be in jeopardy because of what they did outside of work hours. He knew that, but did she?

Strangely, he wanted her more than he could remember ever wanting anyone ever—he wanted to spend a long, lazy time exploring her body, running his hands through her hair and sliding inside her to know how she felt from the inside out. And he desperately wanted to take her away from her responsibilities and give her time to breathe, to relax.

Man, he sounded like a saint, and he wasn't. He didn't even come close. He wasn't being uncharacteristically unselfish. The thought of peace, quiet and hours without talking was deeply alluring. He craved the silence of saying nothing, of allowing his mind to wander, to slow down, to be less than pinprick-focused.

But would she say yes? Would she even agree to his crazy proposition?

No. Maybe. He could only ask. Thank goodness they were alone so that, if Lex shot him down in flames, no one would notice the fireball.

'So, you asked to see me and here I am,' Lex said, crossing her slim leg over her knee. 'Do you need a ride somewhere?'

It was a perfect opening. 'Yes, I do.'

'I wondered how long you would last driving yourself. Cape Town traffic is hellish and, being spread out between the mountains and the sea, it's fairly hard to navigate.'

He'd driven in some of the most dangerous cities in the world and Cape Town was a doddle compared to Manila, Seoul or Mumbai. But he'd allow her to keep thinking he needed her help, especially if he ended up getting his own way. Sometimes, the end justified the means.

'Are you about to tell me that you need me to drive you this weekend?' Lex asked, and he heard the note of excitement in her voice. Then she flushed and looked away. 'You should know my rates triple if I work Saturday afternoon, or on Sundays.'

Cole was pretty sure he could afford whatever she charged. 'Noted.' He wondered what she'd spend the extra money on. He hoped she would buy a new set of tyres for her car and get her brake pads fixed. He heard his phone buzz and saw a notification from Petra, his temporary assistant.

I have booked two nights for you at the famous Aquila Game Reserve, they are expecting you this afternoon.

Right. Damn. He swiped his finger across the screen, punched four on his speed dial and put his phone on loudspeaker. Petra answered immediately. 'Are you happy to go to Aquila Game Reserve, Mr Thorpe? It's one of the best in the country, with incredible amenities. I've booked you a suite—'

'Please cancel the booking.'

He heard her gasp and didn't blame her. He was acting like a spoiled billionaire who couldn't make up his mind. 'My fault, not yours—my plans changed unexpectedly.'

He heard the breath she sucked in. 'Right, okay. But I cancelled your current hotel booking, they've packed up your clothes and they are waiting for you to collect your luggage. The SUV you rented is also waiting for you at the hotel.'

Being picky about his cars, he'd wanted something with a little more grunt, so he'd instructed Petra to find him something hot and exciting to drive.

'Tell the lodge to keep the deposit and I'll rebook for another time,' Cole told her. 'Please book two rooms in Colesberg, and make a booking for two at Rossdale Ski Lodge for two of their best rooms for Saturday and Sunday night.' He looked at Lex and watched her green eyes widen.

There was a good chance she'd say no, and there was always the chance that their crazy attraction would bubble over and scald them both. But that was a chance he was willing to take.

Was she?

CHAPTER SIX

'I'M GOING ON a cross-country road trip to Rhodes, in the Eastern Cape. Would you like to come with me?'

Lex blinked, not sure she'd heard him clearly. He couldn't possibly be asking her to travel halfway across the country, could he? Why? And what, *exactly*, did he want from her? If he assumed, from one hot encounter, that she was going to provide the additional service of warming his bed, boss or no boss, she'd throw the dregs of her coffee in his face.

There were a few very big steps between one hectic kiss and her hopping into bed with him. And that was a journey she hadn't taken for years, five or more to be precise. Acquiring two sisters had played havoc on her dating life and libido.

He saw something in her face or eyes that had him straightening his back, his mouth tightening. 'I'm offering you a job, Lex. It's a twelve-hour drive to Rhodes, and I will need to spend part of that trip working—I do have an international company to run. I will pay you double your normal rate and will cover the costs of your food and accommodation.'

Right, okay. But they couldn't ignore their kiss and their crazy, hot attraction.

'I'm not naïve, Cole, it would be disingenuous to think we'll keep our hands off each other.'

'I love your in-my-face honesty, Lex.'

After a lifetime of dealing with her mother's lies, half-truths and evasions, it was the only way she knew how to operate. 'I prefer honesty to sugar-coated BS.'

'And here it is—I do need to go to Rhodes, I need to inspect this ski-lodge and try to figure out what to do with it, and why my usually sensible father lost his head when making decisions about this property,' Cole said, keeping his tone even. 'It's a long drive to do on your own and you are the Thorpe driver kept on retainer to drive.'

She was.

'But you are also the woman I can't stop think-ing about, and I desperately want to see you naked.'

And there it was, in black and white. 'I'm shocked by the attraction between us. It's strong and intense. And unexpected,' Cole said, spinning his phone on the table before stopping it with his index finger.

Unexpected—that was one way of putting it. She would use other adjectives. Earth-shattering would be one. Other-worldly would be another.

She opened her mouth to speak, but Cole beat her to it. He leaned forward, his hard expression lighten-ing just a fraction.

'Should I have kissed you? The answer is obvious—no. But I did—we did—and we can't change that. Do I want to kiss you again? Yes, of course I do. I know how good we can be together. If one kiss can cause so much heat, then there is no doubt that we would contribute to global warming if we got naked together.' He lifted one powerful shoulder in a shrug. 'We seem to have chemistry. I have no idea where it came from, but I'm not a teenage boy at the mercy of my hormones. If you say no, then it's no.'

He lifted his hands and spread them. 'And nothing that happens between us would affect your job with Thorpe Industries. Yes, if you come with me, there's a good chance we'll end up in bed. But that will always be your choice, and I promise not to pressure you. It will be your call and it's not something you need to decide right now.'

'It's not?'

He frowned. 'No, of course not. Look, if sleeping together is off the table, that's fine and we'll still go to Rhodes as friends. If sex happens, great, and if you decided to sleep with me again, I'd be honoured. If it happens and you don't want to do it again, I'll back off, no questions asked. You hold all the power here, Lex,' he added.

Cole rubbed the back of his neck, as if he were uncertain of his words, whether they were the right ones. 'All I'm asking of you, at this moment, is to come with me, Lex. Step away from real life and let's go on a road trip, forget about reality for a while. Just you and me, the sky and the road. Let's go on an adventure.'

Man, when he put it like that...

Lex asked Cole to give her a moment to think, stood up, walked over to the window and laid a hand on its cold pane. She wasn't naïve. She knew that there was an excellent chance of her ending up in Cole's bed and in his arms. He'd be her first lover in five years, and probably her last for a long time, because when next would she meet a man she felt so attracted to, someone she could imagine being naked with? The men she met were usually married, and the ones who were divorced but single had the heavy baggage of kids of their own and ex-wives. Cole was hot, single and he wanted her.

But he wouldn't push her into doing anything she wasn't comfortable doing. If she decided she was only there in her capacity as a driver, he'd respect her decision and would behave like a gentleman. She trusted him.

And that was strange, because she didn't trust anyone aside from her sisters.

She didn't have to decide about sleeping with him now. He wasn't asking that. All he was asking was to go on a road trip with her. He was offering her the opportunity to leave Cape Town, and her responsibilities, behind.

The girls were away, she didn't have any assignments due or any upcoming exams, her French student was away and Addi would love to have the house to herself.

There wasn't any reason to say no—except, somehow and in some way, she knew that any concentrated time she spent with Cole would change her somehow.

She didn't know how, just that it would.

Lex looked back to see that Cole was working on

his laptop, giving her the time and space she needed. And she couldn't ignore the fact that driving Cole to Rhodes would earn her more than she usually made in six weeks. It was an extraordinarily good deal and it was the opportunity to do what she most wanted: get on the road, drive and clear her head.

She frowned at Cole, wondering if he was taking the long trip for her. No, that was silly, why would he put himself out for her? Sure, he'd kissed her, but he wouldn't change all his plans, take days out of his very busy schedule, to give her the road trip he'd heard she wanted. It was madness to think that way. No, it was just a coincidence. She liked to drive and he needed a driver because he was scared of small planes and helicopters. She squinted at Cole, thinking that such a big, powerful, rugged man didn't look as though he'd be scared of anything.

They couldn't be more different. He was a billionaire who lived in London and had houses and companies around the world, someone who socialised with celebrities, politicians, the pretty and the powerful. She was a twenty-eight-year-old woman who was all but broke, who was trying to give her sisters the stable childhood she'd never had and part-time student who couldn't find enough time to finish her degree. Why was he even attracted to her and she to him?

It made no sense.

Sure, he was a great-looking guy, masculine and attractive rather than simply handsome, with a face and body that demanded a second or third look. And, for some strange reason, he found her, with her intensely freckled face and bright hair, attractive too. And, yes, she really wanted to spend the next few days with him.

But it was dangerous. With him, she felt there was a barrier between her and the world, and whoever wanted to take a piece out of her would have to go through him first, and that Cole would put up a huge fight. She felt protected and feeling that, liking it, was incredibly risky. She was the protector, not the protected.

Lex pushed her hand into her hair and bit down on her bottom lip. She hadn't been looking for him, for any of this. She'd been content in her isolation, in being with the girls, in her woman-dominated world. Because Joelle hopped from one man to another, from one situation to another, she'd learned to protect herself by standing still, by not letting anything or anyone touch her, because she was terrified of letting someone in and having them walk away. She'd mentally distanced herself from anyone but her sisters, keeping her world ultra-small.

But Cole tempted her as no one had before, luring her to explore the world outside her bubble. She felt as if her eyes were opening, her fists were unclenching, her wings unfurling. She didn't like it.

'It'll be okay, Lex, I promise.'

She turned to look at him and saw the almost tender expression on his face, the warmth in his eyes.

'Are you in or out, Lex?'

'I'm in.'

She'd all but agreed to the possibility of having

an affair with a London-based billionaire boss. She hoped she'd made the right decision.

After what seemed like hours of travelling on a dirt road that hugged the curves of a series of mountains, they rolled into Rhodes, a tiny town comprised of a series of pretty Victorian cottages, with Lex behind the wheel. It was only four in the afternoon, but the day was already sliding into twilight, not helped by the massive mountain looming over the town and the low-hanging, dark clouds.

They'd left Cape Town yesterday afternoon and it had taken them for ever to get out of the city. They'd shared the driving and it had been after eleven when they'd rolled into Colesberg. They'd both been exhausted by the long drive in the driving rain and had been unable to do anything but murmur a quiet goodnight before retreating to their separate rooms.

They hadn't kissed again, and Lex missed his lips and wanted his arms around hers. She was deeply conscious of every move Cole made, every breath he took. She looked at his hands, one holding his phone, the other resting on his thigh, eager to have them on her body, his mouth on hers.

Would they make love tonight?

She hoped so.

They had limited time together—she didn't want to waste a minute of it.

On the main street, one of what seemed to be just a few streets in the town, cars were parked nose to nose and bumper to bumper. Down the street, an empty lot held a stage and they noticed a group of people swaying to the sounds of a band. Everyone was dressed for winter weather, except one old man who simply wore a jacket over his pair of shorts. He also wore flip flops on his feet.

Unbelievable.

Seeing a car coming up behind them, Lex indicated to turn left and braked to allow an elderly couple cross the road, both wearing matching yellow beanies. They passed the hood of Cole's car and then, without discussion, turned to walk up to her window. Lex pushed the button to allow the window to drop and pulled up a smile.

'Hi there,' she said, resting her elbow on the windowsill. Damn, it was cold out there.

'Hi, are you the people heading up to Rossdale?'

Lex greeted the couple and nodded, asking them how they knew. 'It's a very small town and all the residents were asked to look out for a fancy car due in around about now.'

'Why?' Cole asked. He leaned towards her window and his face was inches from hers, so close that she could see each long, individual eyelash, a scar on his upper lip and that his eyes held flecks of green. He smelled of the woods and the sea, as fresh and clean as the icy air. Talking about being cold, she wished they'd wrap up this conversation because she was freezing. And, damn, was that a splodge of mushy ice on her windscreen?

'The couple who manage the place left earlier this morning on their way to a doctor. They think Bheki cracked his ankle.' The woman pulled a bright sticky note from her jacket pocket and handed it to Lex. 'They got to town and realised they left their work phone at the resort, so we've been on the lookout for you. Here's the code to the front door. Lerato will try to be back some time mid-morning. You're the only guests.'

Cole pulled back and looked at Lex. 'We can look for a place to stay in town and take a drive up there in the morning.'

That sounded like a plan. She couldn't wait for a hot bath, to get into something warm and to have a decent meal, maybe soup or stew, in front of a roaring fire. A glass of red wine would be her reward for getting them here safely.

'Oh no, dear, you can't do that. The town is full and everyone is booked up.'

'It's either the ski-lodge or a few more hours' drive.' The old man tapped her windowsill. 'You'd better get going, there's snow coming in.'

The couple stepped back from the car, linked arms and ambled across the road and through a cast-iron gate into the brightly lit hotel on the corner.

Lex glanced at Cole, to find his eyes on hers. 'So, what's our next move?' he asked her.

They could either leave, drive to the next town to try and find accommodation or drive up to the very empty lodge. The answer was obvious, but Lex appreciated him asking her opinion. 'The ski-lodge. We're guaranteed a bed there.'

'But we'll be alone,' Cole pointed out.

She got his subtext and knew he was reminding her that there would be no one around to dilute their attraction, or who'd require them to be circumspect. They'd have to face each other and the desire bubbling between them. There would be no place to hide, to run.

His topaz eyes glinted in the low light of the car and Lex shivered, not from the cold but anticipation. She patted his thigh, hoping to lighten the tension in the car. 'It'll be good for you to make your own bed and your own coffee and not be waited on hand and foot.'

Cole covered her hand with his and lifted it to brush his mouth across her knuckles. 'I'll have you know that I make my own coffee all the time,' he quietly told her, his tone low and sexy.

He turned in his seat and grimaced at the clouds building behind them. 'If we're going to go, we should go now. I don't want us driving on an unknown road in the dark during a snow storm. And, damn, I could murder, a whisky.'

'Me too.'

'I like mine in a crystal tumbler, on two cubes of one-inch ice and served on a silver tray.'

It took a moment for her to realise he was teasing and, when she did, she slapped his thigh before starting the car and heading out of town into the night. She flashed her cheekiest smile. 'Thanks, I look forward to you pouring me one.'

Despite the gloom, Rossdale Ski Resort was more impressive than Cole expected it to be. Built of weath-

ered dark timber, steel and stone, it looked modern
but still held a hint of old-world charm.

Having been involved in a few construction proj-
ects himself, Cole didn't want to think about how the
original builders had transported the wood and stone
up the ten-kilometre road he and Lex had just navigated. The road was narrow and there was the occasional drop-off. If a vehicle left the road, it would
land on rocks or in the stream below. Lex, looking
cool and confident, had navigated the road with ease,
allowing the four-by-four slowly to inch its way up
the icy road.

They were on a plateau now, and a couple of buildings sat on the only flat piece of land in the immediate area. The boutique hotel looked like what it
was—a three-storey smallish hotel set on the edge
of another, gentle slope. Off to the other side, at the
bottom of the steepest slope, sat another building,
the offices, a small pub and a shop which hired out
snow equipment. A smallish snow lift stood at the
bottom of the hill.

The slopes looked pretty decent and would give
some good skiing if they received a couple of feet
of snow. He wouldn't get to ski, he reminded himself as Lex pulled the vehicle into an empty parking
bay—one of many. They weren't going to be here
long enough.

He watched Lex remove her hands from the steering wheel and then flex and bend her fingers before
shaking them out. They were trembling, he realised.

Capturing the hand closest to him, he gently

squeezed her fingers before lifting her hand so that he could kiss its tips. 'Hey, are you okay?' Under her freckles, in the cool light of the car her skin was now ashen.

'Just glad that's over,' she told him, emotion in her green, green eyes.

'Glad what is over?' he asked, following her gaze to look over the back seat. 'Are you talking about the road?'

'Well…yes,' she admitted. 'I'm used to urban roads, dodging potholes, passenger buses and pedestrians, not negotiating slippery tracks on the sides of mountains.'

'Have you ever driven a four-by-four before?' Cole asked her.

'I've never driven on a dirt road before,' Lex admitted.

Damn it. If he'd known that he would've taken the wheel at the bottom of the hill when Lex had asked him whether he wanted to drive. He'd wanted to say yes but hadn't wanted to offend her by suggesting that he didn't trust her driving.

'You did well,' he told her, dropping her hand. He looked to the left, to where the triple-storey stone-and-wood structure sat in the ever-descending darkness. 'What do you think?'

Lex leaned forward to look past him and he caught the scent from her hair, lemon and berries, fresh and sweet. 'It looks amazing.'

Cole left the warm car and turned up the collar of his leather jacket, frowning when a splatter of ice hit his nose and then his cheek. He cursed as he walked to the back of the vehicle to pull out their bags.

'The temperature is dropping rapidly, and we need to get a fire started,' he told her. 'Get your pretty butt out of the car, Lex, and let's get inside.'

Lex exited the car and tried to take her bag from Cole but he wasn't having any of it. Putting the strap of his bag over his shoulder, he held her overnight suitcase in his other hand and grabbed her free hand, tugging her through brittle grass to wide stairs leading to a massive front door. Next to the door was a panel and Cole keyed in the code, intensely relieved when the door clicked and opened an inch. Placing his hand on the solid timber, he pushed it open, followed Lex into the house and found himself on a narrow gantry overlooking the double-height common room. Cole dropped the bags and, using the torch app on his phone, found the light switch. One minute they stood in near darkness, the next the hallway was flooded with light.

They had power and, most importantly, he was with Lex. So far, so very good.

CHAPTER SEVEN

LEX DID A full circle of the main house, taking in the
wall lined with vintage skis as decor, and the benches
where people could sit down and remove their shoes.
Not wanting to have to mop the floor, she toed off
her muddy trainers and winced when the cold floor
permeated through the thin layer of her socks. Ignoring her tingling toes, she looked over the railing into
the great room below. The room was huge, with two
fireplaces at each end and leather couches and chairs
grouped around the room, some facing the double-
height window that ran the length of the room. In
daylight they'd have extraordinary views of the mountains, slopes and valleys spreading out below them.

Wow, she thought, placing her hand on the railing that stopped the guests from tumbling to the slate
floor below. She was impressed.

Cole also removed his shoes and she followed him
down the passage, looking around him as he opened
doors. An office, a beautifully appointed bedroom,
another bedroom and what was obviously the master
suite with the same incredible views of the mountains.

There was another set of steps that Cole told her led to the third floor.

'I'm betting this layout is duplicated on the other side of the hall,' he told her as they walked out onto the gantry again. 'Let's see what's downstairs. We also need to get some heat into this place, and I bet we'll find the controls in the kitchen.'

'And food,' Lex said.

'Hopefully,' Cole agreed. She walked down the wide, quite steep wooden stairs, appreciating the way the designer had managed to give the house an essence of sophistication while still keeping the rustic ski-lodge vibe.

'Is this a new build?' she asked Cole.

He looked around. 'Sixty percent of it is. From what I recall from the file Addi handed me containing all the paperwork relating to this place, there was an old farmhouse, double-storey, on this spot. My father kept some walls, removed others and added a floor. Damn, this place looks so familiar,' Cole added.

She stared at his broad back, taking in the way he cocked his head to look at the old stone wall above one huge fireplace. 'I thought you said that you've never been here before,' Lex said, coming to stand next to him.

'I haven't but I feel like I know this house.' Cole pushed a hand through his hair, shook his head and sent her a strained smile. 'Sorry, I'm being ridiculous. I must be hungry and tired.'

Maybe. Or it could be that he did know this house.

Maybe he'd seen photos of it, had heard it described or had visited here as a child and was never told.

But she knew that Cole wasn't interested in discussing his memories or feelings with her, so she slipped past him and walked into the back of the lodge, past the massive dining table, a twenty-four-seater with brightly patterned cushions on the bench seats.

The kitchen was adjacent to the dining area and she stepped into the vast room. It was huge and beautifully designed with large tiles and marble counter-tops. The wine fridge and all the appliances, including an espresso machine, were built in. She looked around, saw an AC control panel and scanned the menu for heating, jabbing her finger against the button. She adjusted the temperature, heard a faint buzz and hoped that within a few minutes—ten or twenty—they wouldn't feel like polar bears walking into an ice shack.

'Great, heat,' Cole said, placing his hand on the counter-top of the free-standing island. 'I don't suppose you've found any food yet?'

'Still looking,' she told him, heading over to the fridge. She opened the doors. As she'd expected, it was filled with fresh vegetables and salads, cheeses and a huge variety of condiments. *Excellent.*

But no milk, she noticed. And that meant no coffee for her, which was problematic.

Curious, Lex walked to the end of the kitchen, saw the entrance to the utility room and stepped inside to see three washer-dryers. Seeing another door, Lex popped it open and released a fist pump, taking in the full to bursting shelves.

There was pasta of all types, cans of Italian plum tomatoes, herbs, spices and various other foods. There were bottles of capers, Asian sauces and spices, vinegars and salad dressings. Seeing a chest freezer in the corner, Lex lifted the lid and saw a series of carefully and beautifully packaged ready meals, soups, stews and curries. There were also frozen beef fillets and tuna steaks, and all types of frozen sea food and—*yay*—frozen milk.

And enough boxes of hand-crafted Belgian chocolates to satisfy Cole's sweet tooth.

She could work with what she'd found.

'Woohoo!' she shouted. 'Cole, we have food— Oomph!'

Lex bounced off Cole's hard chest and the plastic bottle of frozen milk dropped to the floor. It rolled away and Lex ignored it, caught up in the intensity of Cole's yellow-brown eyes. He placed his hand on her hip to steady her and the heat of his hand burned through her clothes into her skin. She didn't need an external source of heat, she just needed to be close to him.

'We've got food,' she told him, annoyed to find she was repeating herself.

The corners of his mouth kicked up. 'I heard. I think the entire valley heard.'

'Sorry, I didn't know you were behind me,' she murmured.

'And yet I am very aware of you, all the time,' Cole stated, his hand coming up to hold the side of her face.

Lex knew she was at a crossroads. She could either stand here and pretend to play it cool, hoping he'd kiss her, or she could give him the green light by making the first move. She was so tired of pulling back, of hiding her attraction, trying not to let him see how much he affected her. She wanted to stop censoring herself, to be herself, for Cole to know the real her for the few days they were together.

She'd promised herself that she'd be completely honest, consistently authentic in her words and her actions, and she wanted him for as long as she could have him. They only had a finite amount of time and, quite frankly, they'd wasted too much of it already.

She also knew there was nothing more between them than a blazing attraction. There was no possibility of a relationship, of a happy-ever-after. She lived in Cape Town and he was based in London but travelled continuously. She wasn't prepared to watch someone she cared for walk away from her, and Cole would definitely do that. And, because she was co-raising her sisters, she couldn't follow anyone anywhere, even if she were asked to do that.

He was her employer. She was his employee.

But none of that mattered, not in this isolated, fabulous boutique hotel on the edge of a mountain deep in rural South Africa.

In this place, it was just Lex and Cole. And Lex very much wanted to get to know Cole in the most earthy, primal way possible. She wanted to be with him—have sex with him—and if she didn't wring every bit of magic out of every second with him she'd regret it for the rest of her life. She couldn't think of anything worse than being old and grey, thinking, *I wish I'd slept with him. I wish I knew what that was like.*

'I'm so attracted to you,' she murmured, her hands on his chest.

'Ditto,' he replied. 'If craving you could be called attraction.'

He craved her? Good to know.

Lex tipped her head back and sent him a long look. Gathering her courage, she swallowed and machine-gunned her next sentence. 'Will you take me to bed? Will you make love to me?'

'Are you sure that's what you want?' he asked her, holding her chin in his big hand.

Lex nodded. 'Very.'

'And you understand—'

'That you can't give me more—not that I asked you to—and that us sleeping together won't affect my job and it's a brief fling in the mountains?' Lex interrupted him. 'Yes, yes and yes.'

Cole wouldn't let her look away. 'It's just that I don't want there to be any misunderstandings later.'

Lex released a very frustrated sigh. 'I get it, Cole. So, unless you want me to sign a damn contract, will you please—I cannot believe I am asking this again— take me to bed?'

She caught the amusement in his eyes, underneath which was a river of desire and anticipation. 'It would be the greatest pleasure of my life, Lex. What's Lex short for, by the way?'

'Yamilex,' she replied, licking her lips. 'It's Arabic.'

'Lex suits you better,' he told her, before pushing a long red curl off her cheek with his finger. She wished he'd kiss her, simply take her mouth so that she'd forget how to speak and think. It had been so long since she'd lost herself in a man's arms and allowed his mouth and hands to spin her away. Lex wound her arms around his neck and pulled a half-smile onto her face. 'So…question.'

'Mmm?'

'Are you planning on seducing me in the pantry? Because I'm pretty sure this luxurious lodge comes with a bed or two.'

Cole wrapped his arms around her waist, lifted her and held her close against his body. He told her to wrap her legs around his waist, and she did, unable to stop herself from placing her lips against his mouth, from sliding her tongue inside his warm heat. He stumbled, just a slight misstep, and he tightened his hold on her.

'I always knew men couldn't do two things at once,' she teased him.

'In a minute, and once I get you horizontal, I'll prove just how wrong you are,' Cole promised her on a sexy growl, walking her out of the pantry and into the kitchen.

When he stepped into the great room, Lex noticed the warmth. He'd lit the fire in the bigger of the two fireplaces and the hiss and crackle of dry wood burning made her smile. That sound, along with rain hitting a tin roof and a howling wind roaring around the house, was one she associated with winter.

Then Lex looked out of the double volume window and gasped. Sleet had turned to proper snow and huge, soft, powdery flakes fluttered down, bright and white against the last of the day's light.

'Cole, it's snowing!' she squealed, pointing to the window. He gave the snow a cursory glance and nodded.

'Yep, well, that's not unexpected.'

'Let's go outside!' she suggested, sliding down his body and hopping from foot to foot. 'I've never seen snow before and I want to know what it feels like.'

'It's cold and wet,' Cole told her, sliding his hands up and under her jersey, his fingers tap-dancing on her ribs and sliding over her breasts. 'I, on the other hand, am hot and dry.'

Right. She really wanted to make love to Cole but… 'The snow might stop and I want to catch a snowflake on my tongue,' Lex told him in an agony of indecision.

'You're kidding, right?' he demanded, incredulous.

She shook her head and winced.

'It's going to snow all night, Lex,' he told her, sounding desperate.

'I know that you think I'm mad, but once me, Addi and the girls, on hearing that the snow would last all day in the Ceres area, drove three hours to find puddles at the end of our trip. The girls cried. Addi and I cursed.' She wrinkled her nose. 'In Africa, when you see snow, you go outside *immediately*. It's a *rule*.'

No matter how tempted she was, no matter how she burned for him, how she couldn't wait for him to make her sigh and scream, she wanted to stand in the snow. The bed, couch, the wall—wherever he wanted to have her—would still be there in ten minutes but the snow might not. 'Ten minutes, Cole. Please?'

Cole looked up at the ceiling and shook his head. 'I cannot believe that we are having this conversation.'

'In the snow versus sex battle,' Lex told him, sounding serious, 'snow is probably always going to win.'

'You Africans are seriously weird.' Cole walked over to the side door leading out onto the patio and opened the door. 'I'm giving you five minutes to catch your snowflake and then I'm getting you naked.'

That sounded like a truly excellent compromise.

Lex caught a snowflake on her tongue and, as soon as she did, Cole covered her mouth with his, tangling his fingers into her hair and twisting his tongue around hers, the snowflake dissolving instantly.

Not expecting to be out for long, they'd left the house in just their jeans and jerseys, and Cole felt the snow landing on his shoulders, in his hair, his body temperature steadily dropping. He knew they should go inside, but Lex's joy in what to him was such a banal weather event had a tiny stream of what he thought might be joy running through his system. For as long as he lived, he'd remember standing out here with her. The vision of Lex catching snowflakes on her tongue, her arms spread out wide, would remain with him until he died.

He felt her shiver and knew that they should return inside as neither of them wore shoes. His socks were wet, and hers would be too, but there was just one thing he needed to do before they went inside.

It was his most recent fantasy, but they didn't know each other well enough for him to ask her to strip in a snowstorm. Pity.

Without warning, Lex whipped her top up and over her head, and she gasped as a couple of snowflakes hit her bare skin. 'Cole, it's freezing!' Lex moaned, hopping from foot to foot.

'You're the one who took her clothes off, you crazy woman. Why?'

Her blazing eyes met his. 'Because you looked like you wanted me to,' she replied. 'And I want you to do whatever you were thinking of.'

'You kill me, Lex,' Cole told her, reaching for the front-facing clasp holding her bra together. 'I just wanted to see you standing in the snow naked. Or half-naked. Lex, you are so very beautiful,' he murmured.

Her torso was long and slim, her breasts bigger than he'd expected and tipped with blush-pink nipples. Freckles covered her skin, fine and the colour of golden syrup, a few shades lighter than the ones on her chest and shoulders. He wanted to kiss every one, but for now he'd be content to lick a snowflake, just one, off her nipple. He felt as if he was commanding nature when a snowflake landed on her breast and slid down her skin. As it hit her nipple, Cole ducked his head and suckled her, his tongue hot against her freezing breast.

He felt her hand come up to grasp his head, her fingers sliding into his hair, and he heard her moan, low, sexy and sweet. Knowing that he couldn't keep her out here for one minute longer, he swung her up in his arms and walked her into the house, kicking the outside door closed with his heel.

Cole walked straight to the area in front of the fire, sighing when the warm air enveloped them. Lex's feet hit the Persian carpet and she turned her back to him, holding her hands out to the fire, utterly unselfcon- sciousness to be standing half-dressed in front of him. He liked that she wasn't shy, that she felt comfortable with him and trusted him enough to take care of her.

And take care of her he would.

Cole dropped her jersey and bra to the floor, bent down, lifted her foot and slid her wet sock off, tossing it to the side. He removed her other sock and, stand- ing up, toed off his own. Then he ran his hands over her slim shoulders and down her long arms to tangle his fingers in hers. Dropping his head, he rested his forehead against hers.

He wanted her, more than he thought was possible. If he was an imaginative man, he'd think she'd cast a spell over him, that he now understood why men crashed onto rocks at the call of a siren, why they launched a thousand ships because of a lovely face.

At this moment there was nothing he wouldn't

do to have her under him, to be inside her, making her his.

But ten minutes in the icy cold might've changed her mind. 'Is this what you still want, Lex?'

Instead of replying, she undid her belt, popped the buttons on her jeans and shimmied the fabric down her legs, before kicking them away. She wore plain white panties, and through the fabric he caught the suggestion of a tidy strip of red hair.

Wrenching his eyes up, he took in her flat stomach, her rounded hips and those stupendous legs. She pulled a band from her hair, shook her head and red curls fell over her shoulders and down her back. He picked one up and gently pulled it straight. If her hair was straight, it would fall to the middle of her back. For some reason, Cole couldn't imagine Lex with straight, smooth hair. It didn't suit her open, vibrant personality.

She was everything lovely, as wild as a summer thunderstorm, as unexpected as a blizzard in Africa—complicated, intriguing, different.

He couldn't wait to explore every inch of her fabulous body, but it was her mind that intrigued him more.

It shouldn't, but it did.

On shedding her jeans, Lex expected Cole to yank her into his arms, lower her to the leather sofa behind them and, well, get busy.

But, instead of hurtling towards the finishing line, Cole just looked at her, taking in her curly hair, her breasts—smaller than she liked—and her too-long legs. His eyes passed over her panties and moved up again, stopping to inspect the small tattoo she had on her right hip. Three, each an inch high, adult elephants encircled two, tiny baby elephants. He paused, and Lex knew he was curious about the artwork.

It wasn't the time for questions and, needing to touch him, to feel connected, Lex reached for his jersey, gently pulling it and the T-shirt he wore underneath up his torso, revealing his wide chest and ridged stomach. After dropping his garments to the floor, she skimmed her hand down his shoulder, down his muscled arms. Her fingers drifted over the back of his hand, slipped between his fingers and he lifted her knuckles to his mouth. His eyes, containing flames of yellow and gold, collided with hers.

'Are you sure about this?' he quietly asked.

She could no more have said no than stop the clouds from releasing snow. 'I'm sure.'

Cole's fingers fluttered over her lips, her cheekbone, the sweep of her jaw. His gentle touch was unanticipated, as sexy as his take-me-away, lust-drenched kisses. She hadn't imagined that such a remote, emotionally unavailable and mentally tough man could be so tender. Cole held her head in his hands, his thumbs sliding over her eyebrows and across her cheekbones.

'I adore your dots, Lex,' he told her, his voice rough with desire.

'Kiss me, Cole,' Lex whispered, raw need in her voice. He lowered his head and his mouth skimmed hers, once, twice, before he covered her lips, feeding her kisses and keeping the tempo sexy and slow.

As they kissed, Lex revelled in the freedom to touch his long, hard body. She trailed her fingers over his chest, down his sides, and walked them across those hard abs. She explored the long length of his sexy hip muscles and ran her finger under the band of his jeans, relishing his groans of appreciation. A slap of power hit her. She could make this man want. She had the ability to make his big body quiver with anticipation. She stroked the tip of her finger along his erection from base to tip and was rewarded by the sound of him sucking in a harsh breath.

'Lex…'

Cole cupped her breasts in his hands, groaning as he buried his face in her neck, sucking on that spot where her neck and shoulder met.

'I need you now,' Cole told her as he hooked his thumbs into her panties and pulled them down. He stared at her thin strip of soft hair, and she gasped as he ran his finger over it. 'So pretty.'

Lex, unable to help herself, widened her legs and heard his harsh gasp as he slid his hand between her legs and his index finger brushed ever so gently over her super-sensitive bundle of nerves. Stars and fireworks exploded on her skin, sensitising her from tip to toe. Her thoughts fled, and she forgot to breathe as his hot finger slipped inside her, followed by another. His thumb swept over her again and Lex felt sexual pressure building. It had been years since she'd been with a man, but she didn't recall sex being this out-of-the-world experience, this exhilarating.

'Cole...'

He'd never in all his life seen anything as sexy as Lex standing in front of the fire, about to orgasm, with snow falling outside. A part of him wanted to watch her as she fell apart, see how her face changed when pleasure hit her, see the wonder in her eyes, watch her skin flush pink under her freckles. But a bigger part of him wanted to be fully and wholly connected with her this first time.

Scooping her up, he laid her on the couch, taking a moment to appreciate her. She looked like femininity distilled: long hair, wild eyes and smooth skin. It took all he had not to rip off his jeans and sink into her, to discover her. Her eyes slammed into his and she lifted her hips in a silent plea to be taken, to be completed. For him to give her what she craved. Before Lex, with those women whose faces and names she'd obliterated from his memory, he'd never taken the time to savour. To discover slopes and valleys, dips and curves. What made a woman scream and what made her sigh.

He couldn't wait to see her fall apart but, first, protection... Digging into his back pocket, he yanked out his wallet, dug around in it and pulled out a condom. Dropping his jeans and underwear, Cole rolled on the condom and placed one hand on the back of the couch, the other on the cushion next to Lex's head, and lowered himself down, keeping his eyes locked on hers. He took a calming breath, knowing that he needed control. But in Lex's eyes he saw impatience, passion, and heard her unspoken plea to be taken on her lips. Her legs fell open and he brushed her entrance, pushing in just a little. Man, she felt amazing.

She whimpered and then sighed his name.

The tips of her long and elegant fingers meandered over the stubble on his jaw. She painted fire on his skin as her fingers skimmed down his neck and danced across his shoulder blades, down his spine and over his butt. Unbelievably, he hardened even further. Unable to wait, Cole lowered his weight and pushed into her with a long, controlled slide.

He covered her mouth with his and the world faded away, entirely focused on where their bodies met. She met him stroke for stroke, her breath deep and sexy in his ear. He held himself rigid, knowing that if he didn't stop she'd be left unsatisfied. *Not acceptable.*

But heat and demand roared through him and his control was on a knife-edge. This was original sin mating, wild, basic, organic, the way it was meant to be. He couldn't wait. He had to move, take, plunder…harder, faster, higher. His breathing increased and his heart threatened to explode…

He heard a whimper, then her groan. Lex clenched around him and his orgasm rocketed through him, chasing hers up, around, through that star, hopping across the moon and sliding down that meteor shower.

When his tour of the galaxy ended, Cole buried his face in Lex's sweet-smelling neck, trying to make sense of their intense physical connection.

She, the sex they'd shared, was the best he'd ever had. Why here? Why now? And why, when it was so very inconvenient?

CHAPTER EIGHT

THIS PLACE LOOKS so familiar.

Thinking back to what he said earlier, Lex dressed in Cole's jersey, swung her legs across his thighs, the backs of her bare legs rubbing against his jeans. Much to her dismay, he'd pulled on his T-shirt.

But, since he'd found a bottle of excellent red wine and two glasses, she was prepared to forgive him.

Lex turned to look behind her and smiled when she saw that it was still snowing. A layer of white covered the brown grass and the patio and she was tempted to get up, get dressed and go and play in the snow. Maybe she could persuade Cole to have a snowball fight with her. Or to make a snowman.

Cole took one look at her face and shook his head. 'I would rather suck my eyeballs out with a straw than go outside,' he told her. Snow wasn't the novelty to him that it was to her.

Lex pouted but Cole remained unmoved.

'I checked the weather forecast earlier and they are predicting more snow tonight. I'm hoping for a few feet so that I can test out some of the slopes.'

'You can ski here?' As soon as the words left her mouth, Lex realised what a stupid question that was. Of course people could ski—it was a ski-lodge. She waved her words away. 'I mean, won't the slopes here be a bit tame for you? In the car, you mentioned that you take a skiing holiday every year, and I can't imagine you doing anything other than the hardest, steepest slopes. What do they call them again—black runs?'

'Why do you assume that I'm good at it?' he asked, amused.

'Because you have an athlete's body.' And because she couldn't imagine Cole being anything but good at things. He was one of life's golden people, both sporty and intellectual. She couldn't see him tolerating failure at anything. He liked control too much to allow that to happen.

'If we get enough snow, I could teach you to snowboard tomorrow.'

Lex shook her head. 'I have the grace and balance of an elephant with an ear infection.'

He laughed. 'You can't be that bad.'

She really was. Lex looked down at his big hand on her thigh—he'd pushed his jersey up to find bare skin—thinking how tanned his hand looked on her pale skin. It was wide, with long fingers ending in short, clean nails. She had a thing about hands, men's hands in particular, and she approved of Cole's.

She especially approved of where he'd put them on her body. They'd made love twice already and, as much as she'd love to indulge in round three, they needed to rest and recuperate, and they needed sustenance. Lex thought about getting up and getting some food, but she was so comfortable sprawled across him.

She recalled Cole's statement about him remembering this house. 'Your father did extensive renovations to this house. It can't possibly look the same, so I'm wondering what's tickling your memory.'

He looked up at the beams crisscrossing the ceiling of the room. 'I feel like I recognise that wall, the fireplace, the slate floors.'

'Did you come here with your father as a child?'

Cole shook his head. 'My father only bought this property about ten years ago and I never went anywhere with my father.'

Lex heard the thread of ice in his voice, a great deal colder than the snow falling outside. '"Never" is a strong word,' she murmured.

'But accurate,' Cole said, seemingly unaware that his grip on her leg had tightened. He wasn't hurting her but the tips of his fingers sank deeper into her flesh. 'My father and I didn't have a relationship. At all, ever.'

Lex skimmed her fingers up and down his bare arm. 'I know how it feels to have a parent who disappoints and lets you down.'

Cole scooted down the couch and rested the back of his head on the couch. 'Oh no, my dad was a great father. Involved, interested, present.'

'But—'

'Just not to me,' Cole clarified.

'I don't understand,' Lex replied.

Cole lifted his hand off his head to push his fingers through his hair. Since she'd done the same earlier, his waves were more pronounced than normal. 'I have an older brother: his name is Sam. He's older by seven years. My father adored him and worshipped the ground he walked on. My parents divorced when I was three or four and I went with my mum, Sam stayed with my dad. Our lives separated from that point onwards.'

They'd split up their family—one child for you, one child for me? To Lex, it sounded so cold and calculated. She'd do anything and everything she could to keep her sisters together, to be a family, but Cole's parents had casually ripped his apart.

'How was your relationship with your mum?'

She hoped it was great and that, unlike her, he'd had one parent he could rely on.

He rolled his shoulders. 'Not bad, I guess. She was there, physically. She fed and clothed me and did those things that mums were supposed to do. I went to boarding school when I was thirteen and, from then on, I only saw her a couple of times a year.'

'Where is she now?'

'She died when I was twenty,' Cole replied in a flat voice.

Lex winced. 'I'm sorry.'

Cole shrugged. 'Sadly, I didn't miss her that much. She was pretty distant and emotionless, to be honest.'

Lex grimaced. He made it sound as if he'd been raised by a robot. Joelle had her faults but the last thing she could be called was emotionless. 'So how often did you see your father? He must've had visitation rights.'

Cole's expression tightened. 'He had them, but he never used them. I don't think I made this clear... from the moment my parents split up, I never had any contact with my father. No calls, emails or visits.'

Cole stood up and headed over to the fireplace, tossing some logs onto the already roaring fire. Lex saw the devastation in his bleak eyes and her heart contracted.

She felt intensely sad for him. While Joelle had, on the whole, been an indifferent mother, they had known affection when Joelle had remembered. Her father had never been in the picture, and Lex knew nothing more about him than his first name. And Joelle wasn't even a hundred percent sure about whether she'd remembered the right guy at the right house party.

Cole's situation with his dad was far more heart-rending. He was constantly reminded that his father didn't want him, and all his life he'd watched his brother have a relationship with their father that he'd been denied, with no explanation. Her heart ached for him.

'How often did Sam see your mum?' she asked.

Cole took his time answering her. 'Once a month, if I remember correctly. Sometimes he spent a week of his school holidays with us.'

That was so sad. Sam had had both his parents while Cole had only had one. 'Do you know why your dad...?' She couldn't find the right phrase to use. Hated him? Neglected him? Cut him out of his life? What type of monster ignored and neglected a child for all of his life?

Cole shook his head. 'I have no idea. I asked my mum, but she always changed the subject or brushed me off.' He lifted his hands and linked them behind his head. 'Not knowing is the killer.'

She instinctively knew what he meant. 'Because it's far better to be hurt by a truth than comforted by a lie,' Lex said.

'Exactly.'

'Being truthful, being authentic and knowing the truth, seeing things clearly, is important to me,' Lex told him. 'I'm really big on seeing things how they are and not how you want them to be.'

Lex waved her words away, conscious she was talking about herself when they'd been talking about him and his childhood. 'Do you think you could be the result of an affair your mum had?'

'It would be an easy explanation except that I am the carbon copy of my father,' Cole replied, blowing her hypothesis out of the water. Cole shoved both his hands into his hair and tugged. 'Why are we talking about this? Surely there's something else we can discuss?'

Lex knew he was done with the heart-to-heart and that she wouldn't get any more from him tonight. And that was fine. These intense discussions were dangerous. It was one thing to explore his body, to find out what made him groan and gasp, but discovering what made him tick, what circumstances had shaped the person he was, was dangerous.

She couldn't afford to become emotionally attached to him. That wasn't something she wanted to do, not when she knew he'd be walking away from her. This was a brief affair, one that would end when they got back to Cape Town.

If they weren't making love then she had to keep their conversation light, skimming the surface. Lex looked up at him through half-closed lids, an expression she'd seen Joelle use a hundred, a thousand, times. 'I've got an idea...' she drawled, dropping her voice in an attempt to sound sexy.

Expectation dashed across his face and his eyes flickered with interest. 'I'm listening...'

She ducked her head so that he couldn't see a hint of her smile. 'There's a freezer in the pantry with some frozen meals. You could take two out and shove them into the microwave to heat.' She arched an eyebrow. 'You do know what a microwave is, right?'

'Funny girl,' he muttered, fighting to hide a smile. He walked over to her, held out his hand and hauled her to her feet.

Then he grimaced. 'At what temperature and for how long?'

Lex rolled her eyes. 'Billionaires, useless at everything but making money,' she teased him.

Cole patted her butt and sent her a satisfied smile. 'I'm good at two things,' he informed her. When she raised an eyebrow, he grinned. 'Making money and making you scream with pleasure.'

She couldn't argue with that.

* * *

The next morning, Lex woke up in the massive empty bed in the biggest of the guest rooms and rolled over, looking for Cole, before remembering that he'd murmured something about…something. Then she'd gone straight back to sleep but, judging by the fact that Cole's side of the bed was still warm, he couldn't have been gone for more than ten or fifteen minutes.

She really hoped he was making coffee.

Lex stretched, pointing her toes and flexing her fingers. Despite having had no more than a few hours of sleep—they'd made love three times during the night but had spent even more time kissing, touching and indulging in some very heavy petting as they'd taken a shower before bed—she felt energised and, yes, happy. Content.

Pretty damn wonderful.

She should enjoy every moment of feeling like this—it was a one-time deal. In a couple of days, she would go back to the predictability of her life, consumed by her need to give her sisters the stability she'd never had. When she returned, she'd go back to putting their needs first.

Here, in the mountains, with the snow still falling and the wind howling, it was all about her pleasure, her wants and needs. And Cole, judging from the way he'd made love to her last night, was determined to give her everything she needed…

Sexually, that was.

He couldn't give her what she craved, what she dreamed about. He'd never be able to make space for her in his life, and space for her sisters, to put her needs first, to be the person she could trust and rely on to be there for her—but that was okay. She was asking a lot and even if he, or any other man, offered, she doubted she'd be brave enough to trust him to do as he promised.

She had love issues, trust issues, being disappointed and being abandoned issues.

Frankly, she was a lot to handle.

Irritated with the longing she felt somewhere deep in her heart, she flung back the covers, walked over to the free-standing club chair and pulled Cole's long-sleeved T-shirt over her head. After shoving her arms into the too-long sleeves, she buried her nose in the neck band, inhaling his scent. She had to find out what cologne he used—it was super-sexy and, oh, so Cole. She closed her eyes, lifted his shirt over her mouth and breathed deeply again.

'Are you having a relationship with my shirt?'

Her eyes flew open to see Cole standing in the doorway, holding two cups of coffee, amusement dancing in his eyes. He wore black, straight-legged track pants and a fresh, long-sleeved cream T-shirt that fell down his chest and over his stomach. It also highlighted the muscles in his big arms.

She dropped the neck of the T-shirt, wishing she could control her blush. 'I just like the way you smell,' she admitted.

'Good to know,' he told her, walking towards her and holding out a mug. Lex gratefully accepted the mug and wrapped her hands around it. She jumped a little when Cole dropped a kiss on her head, unused to casual affection and surprised to realise how much she liked it.

Feeling a little embarrassed, Lex walked over to the tall window and looked down the valley, which was covered in a thick layer of snow. It looked like a Christmas card, the snow a glittering white carpet. 'Wow.'

'There's a better view from the adjoining sitting room.' Cole nodded to the door to her right. Lex walked through into a room with two glass walls forming the corner of the room and giving them a one-eighty-degree view of the valley spread out below them. A white lounging bed sat diagonally across the corner, and Lex could see herself lying there with a blanket over her knees, watching the snow drift past. Or sleeping with a puppy tucked into her legs, or lying there naked, her hand on her belly, swollen with a baby...

Longing swept over her, not so much for the gorgeous room in a lovely hotel, or for the view. It was a longing for what she couldn't have, what she wouldn't have for years, if ever: peace, tranquillity, quiet... *stability*. Time on her own, a life of her own. A baby and a place of her own...

What was wrong with her? It was a room—one of the nicest she'd ever seen, but still a room—and not a dream chamber!

Cole walked into the room and sat down on the edge of the lounger, and when she joined him there he put his free hand on her knee. 'That's some view,' he admitted. 'This is a very pretty place.'

Lex leaned into him just a little. 'My sisters would love this,' she admitted. Yes, she'd told herself she wouldn't think about them, but they were a huge part of her life and she couldn't help it.

They were a part of her and always would be.

Cole half-turned to face her. 'Tell me how you came to have them, Lex. In fact, go back further...'

'That's a long story,' she murmured, wanting to open up but scared that she'd tell him more than she should, more than she'd told anyone before.

He lifted his coffee cup. 'This is a big cup of coffee and I'm not going anywhere until it's done.'

Well, then. She looked out of the window and wondered where to start. 'I told you how they came to live with us, how much of a free spirit my mum was.' She wrapped her hands around her mug and sipped. 'We bounced from house to house, depending on what boyfriend was willing to house her, her blonde-haired angel and her red-haired brat. Life with Joelle was... unstable.'

Cole held up a hand. 'Wait, back up. What did you mean by that "red-haired brat" statement? Did your mother not like your looks?'

'Not liking my looks was a very tame way of putting it,' Lex said, trying to keep her tone level as old hurts washed over her. Still after all this time, despite the work she'd done to come to terms with Joelle's cruelty, she felt small and vulnerable.

'Tell me, Lex.'

'When I was five, she told me that my face looked like someone had thrown dirt at it and stained it. By six, I suspected I was ugly. By seven, thanks to Joelle's comments, I believed I was.'

'The last thing you are is ugly, Lex,' Cole informed her, his voice hard and tinged with anger. Not at her, but at her mother and her casual cruelty.

'I know that now. But, when you are a young child with bright-red hair and a face full of freckles, when you look so very different, it's easy to believe what you are told. Especially when your mother constantly tells you how pretty your blonde sister is, and how angelic she looks. I was bullied at school. I had no friends and I wanted to be anyone but me.'

'Go on, Lex.'

Lex tapped her finger against the cup. 'So, one summer holiday, Joelle decided that it was time to dye my hair. We had no money, so she bought a cheap dye kit which turned my hair neon-orange. Tom, Storm's dad, sent me money to go to the hairdresser and the choice was to either dye my hair blonde or shave it off. I went for blonde and I remained a blonde for the next decade or so. I also used foundation to cover my freckles. My efforts paid off because my mum started calling me pretty.'

Cole released a low growl, picked up a bright curl, wound it around his finger and rubbed the ends between his fingers. 'Obviously that phase ended. What changed?'

She lifted her mug to her mouth, took a sip and

smiled. 'Actually, that relates to your original question about how Nixi and Snow came to live with us.'

'I'm listening,' Cole assured her again and everything about his body language said that he was. His eyes didn't leave her face and his hand on her thigh was a connection she badly needed. 'Long story long...when I was sixteen and Addi seventeen, Joelle dumped us with a great-aunt and forgot to collect us, which was a blessing in disguise. Addi and I adored Aunt Kate and we loved living with her. Shortly after I turned twenty-one, Aunt Kate died of a massive heart attack, but she left her house to Addi and me.'

'Giving you the stability, you craved,' Cole murmured.

How did he know that? How was he able to hear what she didn't say?

Feeling bewildered, she continued. 'We rented rooms in the house to other students and their rent paid our living expenses. Aunt Kate also had a small life insurance policy, but it was only enough to cover the fees for one of us to attend university. Addi is a lot more academic than I am—she's quite brilliant, in fact—so we decided that she would study full-time and I would work and study part-time. Then, when she got a high-paying job, she would help me to pay for my degree. That was the plan...'

'But?'

'But Joelle returned to Cape Town with the girls. Suddenly we were responsible for two little girls who were confused and lost. Luckily, Addi had just graduated and was offered a great job by your dad. She had the money to support us, but there wasn't enough to pay for day care. I had plans to go to university full-time, but someone needed to look after the girls, to do the cooking and the cleaning.'

'And you were how old?' Cole asked.

'Twenty-three.'

'That's young to take on that much responsibility.'

But what else could they have done—sent the girls into foster care, or back to Joelle? Keeping them had been the only decent option.

'Finish the story, Lex.'

Lex shrugged, confused. 'That's it.'

He shook his head. 'You haven't explained how you went from being a bottle blonde to embracing your red hair and freckled face.'

Oh, *that*. 'As you saw, Nixi is olive-skinned with black hair—I think her father might be from India or one of the island countries. Snow looks like me. You do know that red hair is a mutant gene, right?'

'You are not a mutant,' Cole emphatically stated. 'I think your hair is gorgeous, as are your freckles.'

Lex smiled at his immediate, and sweet, response. 'Anyway, to get red hair and freckles, and if neither parent is ginger, they both need to carry the gene and pass it on. So, Joelle is partly responsible for my much-hated hair, a fact I occasionally remind her of.'

'So you do speak to her?'

'We only started speaking to her again a few months after the girls came to live with us. We nag her to talk to Nixi and Snow, so that they have *some* contact with her. We don't have much to say to her, and Addi tends to do the communicating, because I lost it with her about eighteen months ago.'

'What happened?'

'I caught Snow putting my foundation all over her face and over everything else. She told me she hated her hair and that she wanted to cover her dots, like I did. My heart stopped—because she's beautiful, so beautiful, Cole.'

'As are you,' he softly murmured.

Lex had to ignore him or else she'd never get her words up and through her tight throat. 'Joelle told her, just like she told me, that she had dirt on her face and that her hair was ugly. I was so angry, Cole. I told her she was beautiful, that she was unique and lovely and wonderful—' Lex heard her voice crack. 'She just looked at me and asked me why she should believe me when I covered my freckles, when I dyed my hair.'

Cole sucked in a sharp breath. *'Sweetheart.'*

'I realised that I couldn't let Joelle destroy her as she destroyed me and that I had to walk the walk as well as talk the talk. I washed the foundation off my face and went to the store, grabbed a bottle of dye that was closest to my natural colour and dyed it back to red. And I promised Snow, promised myself, that I would never be anything but authentically me.'

'That's incredible, Lex—you're incredible.' The sincerity in his eyes and on his face made her throat close up. 'And is your sister embracing her looks too?' he asked.

Lex released a low chuckle. 'She's a flaming diva, in every way that counts. And she isn't being bullied at school, and I'm grateful for that. But that could be because she's Nixi's sister.'

'She's popular?'

'She's eight, so whatever popular means at eight. Nixi is a strong character. She's either going to become a world leader or lead her own gang.'

Cole's deep laugh filled the car. 'They sound… interesting.'

'Interesting, frustrating, stubborn. Sweet.'

He squeezed her knee again, keeping the pressure until she looked at him. 'Just like their half-sister. And Lex?'

Her heart, stupid thing, missed a couple of beats at the warm flames she saw in his gold eyes. 'I'm very glad you're not a blonde any more. You wouldn't be you without your bright hair and million-plus dots. Oh, and I also think your body is pretty fabulous and I love…' He stopped speaking to pull back the band of the shirt she wore to kiss her shoulder.

What did he love…what? He wasn't about to say something weird, was he? They'd only slept together once and this was supposed to be a brief fling, not anything serious. But what if he did? How would she answer? What could she say?

He lifted his head to grin at her. 'I love the fact that you know your way around a microwave. You wouldn't happen to know your way around a frying pan, would you? Because the housekeeper can't get back because of the weather. I saw bacon in the freezer and pancake mix in the pantry…'

Breakfast.

He was talking about food.

Getting a bit ahead of yourself there, weren't you? Idiot.

CHAPTER NINE

THE NEXT DAY, Cole stood by the huge windows of the great room, his hands wrapped around a cup of coffee, and stared at the white landscape in front of him. It was exceptionally cold, and the clouds hung low in the sky, threatening to dump another batch of snow onto the three or so feet they'd received the night before.

Cole wasn't familiar with winter in the Eastern Cape, but this amount of snow seemed excessive. He heard movement in the kitchen and the sound of Lex singing. It took him a while to recognise the chorus because Lex couldn't hold a tune. Sitting down in one of the huge leather chairs, he rested his ankle on the opposite knee, happy for some time on his own.

What had possessed him to spill his secrets to Lex, to run his mouth? He'd told her more about his family situation than he'd told anyone, and he felt angsty and irritable. She was someone he was having an ultra-brief affair with—she wasn't a girlfriend. She barely qualified as a friend.

So why then had he rambled on and on?

Cole rubbed the back of his neck, wincing when his cold fingers touched the skin under the collar of his shirt. Lex was temporary, a transient attraction…

Why was he spending so much time convincing himself that she meant nothing to him, reminding himself she was leaving his life? Was he doing that because a part of him—the same part that had trusted her with his hurt and confusion around his family—wanted her to stick around, to be a part of his life going forward?

He couldn't sustain a relationship with her. He knew he'd bail when he got into waters that were deeper than he liked. A decade ago, he'd had a series of relationships, none of which had worked out. He simply wasn't any good at them, and within a couple of months he felt as if he had a noose around his neck, all the life and air being squeezed out of him. Some of his previous lovers had offered everything they had, love and acceptance, fidelity and adoration, but it had never felt as though it was enough.

Cole knew, with complete certainty, that he was the problem, not them. He was unable to receive love and, because his failures hurt other people, he'd vowed to keep his relationships shallow and short.

He ran at the first demand of commitment and the tiniest hint of emotional intimacy as soon as a woman started asking for more. The chances were high that he'd do the same thing if he tried to have a relationship with Lex.

He knew that however much he was offered—a woman could hand him her heart on a velvet cushion—it would never be enough. They'd never be able to fill the hole his father's neglect had left in his life.

And, even if Lex was the one person who could make him feel whole—which was a stretch, but this was a mental exercise and not a lifelong commitment—a relationship between them could never work.

He'd always avoided single mothers and couldn't see himself being a stepdad. He hadn't been given the opportunity to be Grenville's son and had no reference point on how to be a father. And, if continuing his affair with Lex were an option, he'd have to share the little time he had with Lex with her sisters. Not ideal.

Ifs, buts, whats, hows… He sighed. A couple of days, that was all they had, the only commitment he could make.

Lex crossed the great hall to him and held up her phone. 'I don't have any signal,' she told him. 'And the power has just gone out.'

That wasn't a surprise. Power and communication were always the first to go in weather events.

'This place will have a generator,' Cole told her. 'There is no way that my father would spend millions on decor and not have a backup plan if the lights went out. It should come on in a few minutes.'

He'd barely finished his sentence when the rumble of the generator drifted over to them and the lights in the great room flickered on.

Lex sat on the arm of his seat and, thinking she was too far away, Cole wrapped his arm around her and pulled her onto his lap. She sat at right angles to him, her back against one arm of the chair, her legs draped over the other. Happy to have her close, he ran a hand over her bright head.

Lex took his mug out of his hand and took a sip. 'It's so beautiful. It looks like someone sprinkled icing sugar everywhere. The girls would love this place and would adore the snow.' She handed him a small smile. 'I feel a bit guilty that I am here without them.'

Cole picked up his phone, researched some flights and distances, did some mental calculations and looked at his watch. 'It's shortly after nine. If we all hustle, we could probably get them here by mid-afternoon.'

Lex stared at him, a frown pulling her eyebrows together. 'What are you talking about?'

'A private plane from Durban to East London, a helicopter from East London to here. We could send them back tomorrow.'

Where were these words coming from? Hadn't he just admitted to himself that he wasn't prepared to share his time with Lex with anyone else? But he'd seen the yearning on her face and had instinctively wanted to make her happy.

Her mouth fell open and he used his knuckle to lift it close. 'If they want to see snow, I can make that happen.'

'It would cost a fortune!'

He shrugged, prepared to spend whatever he needed to. 'Well?' he asked, when she didn't say anything.

She wrinkled her nose and, after another minute of thinking, shook her head. 'It's a lovely offer, Cole, and I so appreciate it…but we couldn't put you to that trouble and that expense.'

'I'm offering,' he pointed out.

'Thank you, but no.

'I appreciate you thinking of them—it was very sweet of you,' she added in an ultra-polite voice. She didn't sound like herself at all. And sweet? He was anything but.

Lex rolled off his lap and stood up, jamming her hands into the front pockets of her jeans and hunching her shoulders forwards. She wore a russet-coloured jersey and fluffy socks on her feet.

He sat up, reached forward and hooked his finger in the band of her jeans, pulling her to where he sat. He pulled her back down to his lap and sighed when she sat on his thighs, her back ramrod-straight, her hands between her knees.

Why did she look so miserable, so guilty? He re-membered hearing that she hadn't had any time away from them in five years. 'It's okay to say no, Lex.'

She turned her head to look at him. 'This is the first time I've had concentrated time on my own since they arrived five years ago. This is my little holiday, my time to decompress, to simply be. I don't want to be interrupted by someone asking me for milk or juice or how snow is made. I don't want to have to supervise meals and bath times and read six stories before they go to sleep. I just want to be here, with you, isolated and quiet. For a few days, I just want to be me,' she told him.

Fine with him. He didn't have a single objection to anything she was saying.

'But I feel so damn guilty for turning down such an amazing opportunity for them to be overawed by the helicopter ride, to play in the snow. They've had so little, Cole—we haven't been able to give them much.'

He stroked his hand up and down her slim back. 'No, only a stable house, food, the chance to go to the same school every day and sleep in the same bed every night.'

He leaned down to kiss her temple. 'And don't forget love and affection, Lex—you've given them a lot of that. They are very lucky girls.'

He'd been raised with every toy, been given the best education and had always worn designer clothing but he'd have swapped all of it in a heartbeat for a kiss goodnight, someone to read him a story, to nag him about bath and bed times. Lex had no idea how valuable her gift to her sisters was.

Lex released a huge sigh, the tension flowed out of her body and she leaned sideways to rest her head on his chest, curling into him. 'I feel so damn guilty, Cole,' she whispered.

'For what, sweetheart?'

'For resenting them, for being angry because I've sacrificed so much for all of them. For being jealous of Addi,' she added, so quietly he almost didn't hear her.

He encircled her body with his arms, keeping

her clasped to his body. 'Do you want to explain that, Lex?'

'No.'

It was an honest and forthright answer and not unexpected. 'C'mon, Lex,' he coaxed her, partly because he was curious about this woman, but also because he sensed she needed to talk to someone.

'When we were young, I loved her to death and she was my best friend—but I was angry because she was born blonde and beautiful and I wasn't. She's so very smart and so effortlessly lovely.'

Sure. But Lex's sister hadn't generated a spark of desire in him while Lex sparked an out-of-control wildfire.

'When we were kids, I always felt like I was a step or two behind her, constantly trying to catch up. I thought that would change when we became adults but, even then, Addi always came first.'

'Give me an example,' Cole prompted.

'How many do you need?' Lex asked with a snort-laugh. 'She got her degree first. I went out to work. I was going to go to uni when the girls arrived, but I had to stay home and look after them while Addi went out to work. I haven't had a moment to myself lately because Addi's been haring around Africa staying in your fancy hotels as she shows Jude Fisher around.' She pulled away but he wouldn't let her.

'Go on.'

'I feel like I'm the one who's made the majority of the sacrifices, who's always got the short end of the stick. I gave up my career, my love life, my student life, my degree, to look after the girls. Sometimes I feel like Cinderella, and that my sisters have had an easier ride than me. That I am the one who's always going to be expected to make the sacrifices.'

She pushed away from him and pushed the balls of her hands into her eye sockets. 'And I hate feeling like that, hate feeling cross and resentful and jealous. I love them, Cole.'

'Of course you do,' he told her. 'You can still love them and feel angry, Lex. You are allowed to feel two emotions at once.'

She nodded. 'But I sound like I'm whining, and I hate whiners. You have to play the cards you are dealt and simply get on with it. But, now and again, I'd like to be at the top of the list of priorities, Cole. Just once.'

He stared at her lovely profile and his heart rate kicked up just a little. She'd done so much for so many people and she was beating herself up for some very normal feelings. She was, bar none, one of the strongest people he'd ever met. He could juggle numbers, make billion-dollar decisions without turning a hair and fly down steep ski-slopes but, if two half-siblings dropped into his life, he wouldn't know what to do with them or how to raise them.

And he was thirty-six, not in his early twenties. She'd have his respect for ever for doing the hard stuff. And, yeah, she was occasionally allowed to feel resentful and jealous. He was just surprised she didn't feel those emotions more often.

He watched as she pushed her hands into her hair and twisted the curls, making some sort of messy bun on the top of her head which she secured with the hair band she wore on her wrist.

She sighed and looked out at the snow. 'Despite wanting to be here with you, on our own, I'm still very tempted to take you up on that offer to give the kids a helicopter ride, to allow them to play in the snow. It would be a dream come true for them, and they'd remember it for the rest of their lives.'

He forced a grimace. 'I might've got a bit carried away with that offer, sweetheart. I don't think the helicopters would be able to fly when there's a chance the weather will close in.'

It wasn't a complete lie. The reports said that another system was moving in and more snow was expected.

'Are you just saying that to make me feel better?' Lex asked, looking suspicious.

Of course he was. He'd do anything, say anything, pay anything to take the misery out of her eyes. 'No.'

She smiled at him, sliding her hand up and down his chest. 'Liar. But thank you.' Lex settled back down and they both stared out of the window, enjoying the snow-covered slopes, the stillness of the morning punctuated by the low hum of the generator. This lounge, and the deck outside, was a great place to sit and watch the skiers while enjoying a cup of *glühwein* or whisky-laced hot chocolate.

Cole gestured to the ski-slope to their left. 'I'm going to tromp down there shortly. I can't come to a ski resort I own—or temporarily own—and not ski.

There's a rental shop within the office buildings. I'll find all the equipment I need there.'

'You're going to have to figure out how to get the ski lift working or else it's going to be a long, wet hike up that hill,' Lex told him, smiling.

'I'll figure it out,' Cole told her. 'When I'm done, maybe I can teach you how to ski.'

Lex sent him a look full of humour-coated desire. 'I could think of something I'd much rather do with you than learn to snowboard.'

'That's so incredibly tempting.'

Cole ducked his head to kiss her but pulled back at the last second. They'd had two intense conversations—one last night, one a minute ago—and they needed some distance, a little bit of space. This was getting too deep, too fast, and it pushed him out of his comfort zone.

'If I kiss you properly, I'll be tempted to take you upstairs instead of hitting the slopes.'

Lex sat up and he could feel her pulling back as her many shields came up. 'I'm sorry I dumped on you. I know that wasn't part of our no-strings fling.'

He frowned, puzzled by her statement. He'd opened up to her, had exposed himself, and he didn't feel the need to apologise. Why did she? 'We can be friends as well as lovers, Lex.'

She wrinkled her nose and shrugged. 'I guess.' But she didn't look convinced. He felt the need to reassure her. 'There isn't a rule book we need to follow.'

She patted his chest and climbed off his lap. 'It would be so much easier if we did,' she quietly said before pulling up a smile. 'I'm going to have a nap while you play in the snow.'

His eyes sparked with interest and Lex smiled, her good humour restored by the interest she saw in his eyes.

He wanted her, she wanted him…nothing more, nothing less.

It was one sentence and the only rule they needed to follow.

Who needed a book?

Cole came to a controlled stop at the bottom of the run and placed his hands on his thighs, pulling in deep breaths of icy air. He turned and looked up the slope, called, according to the map in the shop, Charlie's Run, and nodded, satisfied. His thigh muscles burned from the three treks he'd made up the ski-slope through the snow carrying his board but flying down the slope was always worth it.

Cole bent down to release his feet from the snow-board and wondered who Charlie was and why the name popped up all over the resort. The small pub with a deck overlooking the ski-slopes was called Charlie's, this run was called after Charlie and the subsidiary company of Thorpe Industries that owned this ski resort was called Charlie On The Mountain. A stupid name for a company but, obviously, one that had held some significance for Grenville.

Was Charlie the name of a lover, an old friend, a dog his dad had loved? Because he had no insight into his father's life, and had never met the people who were important to him, he didn't know.

But he could ask. Cole pulled his phone out of a zippered pocket in his ski-jacket and opened up his email application, banging out a quick message to Sam's lawyer.

Who is Charlie? Why is everything at the ski resort Grenville owned named after him? Can you ask Sam and get back to me?

There were rules about how much contact Sam had with the outside world and Cole knew that he might not get an answer. And, if he did, it might be in a few weeks' or months' time. Or never.

Cole picked up his snowboard and tucked it under her arm, debating whether to climb the slope again. He loved to exercise, loved the hitch in his breath, feeling his muscles burning and perspiration rolling down his spine—and his body felt tight after all that driving.

Sex was great, but it wasn't great exercise.

Sex with Lex was better than great, he admitted as he pushed his hand through his damp hair. Did he have time for another run? he wondered, glancing at the bank of black clouds in the distance. They were calling this system the biggest snow event of the past fifty years and those dark clouds moving in held more snow. He had maybe an hour left before it started to snow again. This would be his last ride for today.

Besides, he couldn't wait to get back to Lex.

Despite only catching a few hours' sleep last night, he'd slept well, and deeply. He generally preferred to sleep alone but he loved having her in his bed. Wrapping his arm around her waist and anchoring her to him felt right, completely natural.

When he'd woken up, she'd been in the same position. Having her there, her butt tucked into his bent legs, his hand holding her breast, was where she was meant to be. But then she'd wiggled and all thoughts had been obliterated as his body had come to attention and his brain had shut down.

She was as alluring out of bed as she was in it. He'd been surprised by her opening up this morning, pleased but surprised. But, as soon as they'd ended the conversation, she'd pulled back and he'd sensed that she regretted being so open and honest about her thoughts and feelings. Why? She'd had a rough few years, and she'd played the game with the chips she had. If she occasionally felt bitter, edgy, resentful, she had the right. She'd made huge sacrifices for her sisters.

He admired her and respected her more. He was a child of extreme privilege, and had had every opportunity. While he'd worked extremely hard to set up a successful company, he'd been afforded the time to get his degree, and had been able to give his entire focus to his studies, and afterward to his company. He'd always had money, but Lex was juggling her sisters, her degree, a part-time job and making ends meet.

And she felt bad because occasionally she felt

guilty about taking some time for herself, resentful about what she'd been forced to sacrifice. She was, frankly, one of the strongest, best people he'd ever met.

At the top of the slope, he slipped his feet into his mounts, tightened the clasp and rocked the board back and forth. Instead of seeing the snow-covered slope, he saw Lex's lovely face, her bright hair on his white pillow, her slim, sexy body, and thought that he couldn't wait to get back to her, to lower her to the rug in front of the fire. Or to simply share a cup of coffee or glass of wine with her, happy to listen to tales of her busy, girly life.

Cole sighed, annoyed with himself. They were having an affair, he reminded himself. A temporary fling, something that was only built to last a few days for as long as they were here at Rossdale— or maybe, if he could talk her into it, for as long as he was in South Africa. There was nothing between them but sex...

But, damn, a small part of him wished there could be.

Cole rocked the board, the snowboard slipped over the lip and he started to gather speed. He was at a pretty high altitude, he realised, that was why his brain was scrambled. There wasn't enough oxygen to power his brain. When he got back to Cape Town, things would go back to normal.

He hoped.

Because if they didn't, he was in big trouble.

CHAPTER TEN

'WE HAD AN extraordinary amount of snow already, and they are forecasting more tonight,' Cole told Lex as he poured her a glass of red wine.

They were in the kitchen and Cole stood next to her at the kitchen island, watching her as she threw together a simple pasta dish of garlic, capers and anchovies.

'When I got back this afternoon from snowboarding, I jumped onto my computer and managed to find the town's social media page,' Cole continued. 'Rhodes is cut off and no one is getting in or out for the next few days. They've had reports of damaged homes and businesses already and, apparently, there's more to come.'

Lex bit her lip. They were higher up the mountain and were probably going to see more snow than everyone else. Would the ski-lodge be able to cope with what was coming? Cole placed a hand on her butt and gave her a reassuring pat. 'We might not be leaving any time soon but we'll be fine.'

Lex lifted the glass of wine to her lips, thinking

that he was good at reassurance. He'd managed to convince her that exposing the fear and resentment about raising her sisters, and the sacrifices she'd made, was normal.

It was nice to unburden herself, to feel emotionally connected to a man, but she couldn't allow it to happen again. He'd been there this time, but he wouldn't be there in the future. She couldn't make opening up, sharing her inner world, a habit. Cole wasn't going to stick around.

Even if he did live in Cape Town and wanted more from her, he'd run when confronted with the day-to-day reality of her life. She was her sisters' primary care-giver and they'd be a huge part of her life—the biggest part—for the next ten to fifteen years. Cole, or any other man, would have to be able to accept the package deal: Lex and her four sisters, two of whom would live with her until they were grown.

Yeah, her baggage would fill one of those massive cargo planes that carried tanks and helicopters—Cole wasn't even interested in a relationship, so he would never be prepared to help her carry hers. And, that being the case, she shouldn't open up to him, let him in.

It would make saying goodbye a thousand times harder than it needed to be.

No, she couldn't watch another person she loved walk away from her—not again. Her heart had been kicked around enough, thank you.

'We have wood, food and lots of fuel for the generator,' Cole reassured her, pulling her back to the present.

'I'm not worried,' Lex told him. Well, she wasn't worried about the snow storm. Allowing herself to get close to him, to feel more than she should? Yeah, she was worried about that.

'What else did the local media have to say?' Lex asked him.

Cole straightened and frowned. 'They have people missing and a town that is packed to capacity, people who are stranded.'

Lex's head snapped up. 'They have people missing?'

'Yeah. Two shepherds haven't checked in, and they can't contact them on their phones. They're assuming their batteries have died.'

'Have they sent their S and R team out?' Lex demanded.

'Search and Rescue? It's a small town, Lex, they don't have the resources. But I did call the number I found online and spoke to a guy who's coordinating their disaster management team. I offered to hire a helicopter to search for them and said that I would cover the costs to bring in an S and R team.'

Or course he had. Whether it was a life-or-death situation, or giving her sisters a treat of playing in the snow, he was so quick to offer his help, to use his money. Lex respected that. What was the point of having so much money if you didn't use it to help others?

'That's good of you, Cole. What did they say?'

Cole frowned. 'They appreciated the offer, but all helicopters and planes are going to be grounded shortly. The authorities don't want anyone flying, as the next cold front is moving in very quickly.'

So, even if she'd wanted to take Cole up on his very generous offer to bring the girls here to play in the snow, the weather wasn't playing ball, which allowed Lex to release the last vestiges of guilt at denying her sisters an awesome treat.

It was still going to be Cole and her alone in this big house. Excellent. Then she remembered that men were caught in the snow and felt ashamed of herself.

'The coordinator said that he was hoping the shepherds got to one of the huts they have at higher altitudes. If they did, there are enough supplies in the huts to keep them warm and fed,' Cole explained.

'And the sheep?' Lex asked. She couldn't stomach the idea of the animals freezing to death.

'I asked about them too, and apparently the herders love their animals and the huts have enclosed shelters to house the flock. Apparently, they are hardy men who know these mountains and how unpredictable the weather can be. He was cautiously optimistic.'

Lex nodded, relieved.

'How old is this place?' Lex asked him, changing the subject as she stirred the sauce.

'The original structure is over eighty years old,' Cole told her, resting his arms on the island. 'Maybe Charlie was the original owner of Rossdale Ski Resort.'

Cole explained how so many things at the resort were named after 'Charlie' and that he'd been wondering who this Charlie person was.

'It could be anyone,' Lex told him, wrinkling her nose.

Cole grimaced. 'I know. But the name is everywhere, so I'd like to know why my father felt the need to name everything after this person.' He explained that he'd sent an email to his brother's lawyer but wasn't expecting a reply soon, if one came at all.

'You don't sound very optimistic,' Lex commented.

Cole stared into his ruby-red wine. 'Sam and I have a complicated relationship. I saw him when he visited our mother, but I veered between worshipping him—he was a lot older and cooler—and being incredibly jealous and resentful because he had a relationship with Grenville and I didn't. We haven't had contact for fifteen years so the chance of a quick response, or any response, isn't good.'

Lex grimaced. She knew how important siblings could be and couldn't imagine her life without her sisters. Addi was her first and last best friend. They were a solid team, and they had each other's backs, no matter what. The sky could fall in and sea levels could rise but she and Addi would build a boat, make a plan…together.

'Why is that?'

Cole didn't elaborate on his comment so Lex gently kicked his ankle with her sock-covered foot. When he couldn't look at her, her heart plummeted to her toes. 'What happened with your brother, Cole?' she asked.

He walked around the island and picked up the

cork to the wine bottle, tossing it from hand to hand. 'We were never close but we did keep in contact after he left school and went to uni,' he explained. 'Then one day—I was in my late teens—he stopped answering my calls, nor did he return my emails. I went over to his flat and I sat on his steps every afternoon for two days until he appeared. I demanded to know what his problem was.'

Lex placed her elbows on the island, morbidly fascinated. 'What did he say?'

'Nothing. He told me that a relationship between us was impossible.'

'Why would he do that?'

'Because my father ordered him to and Grenville's word was law. If Sam wanted to be his son, inherit his fortune, be the next Thorpe to run the family business, then he had to cut me out of his life.'

'But why? That makes no sense.'

'It made sense to Grenville. And, when Grenville died, I was not mentioned in his will. He left everything to Sam.'

Wait, hold on. Lex knew that he owned Thorpe Industries. She'd seen the company memo stating that Sam Thorpe had retired and that Cole was now the main shareholder and CEO of Thorpe Industries, the holding company with hundreds of smaller businesses under its wing. How had that come about if his brother had inherited everything from their father?

Cole explained about Sam renouncing his material possessions to become a monk and how he'd passed all his assets over to him.

'I was on my way to acquiring their company, about to launch a hostile takeover. When I had their attention, when they had to deal with me, I was going to demand answers from my father and have that showdown I thought I needed. All I ever wanted was for them to see me, acknowledge me.' Cole stared out of the window into the stygian night. 'But my father pre-empted me from having any sort of closure by dying, and then Sam pulled this crazy stunt of passing everything over to me. I wish…'

His voice was laced with pain, making his words sound scalpel-sharp. 'What do you wish, Cole?' she asked softly.

He placed his hands on the island and stared down at the tiled floor. When he spoke, his words were so low that she had to strain to hear them.

'I wish I knew what I did to make him hate me so.'

There was pain in his voice, also confusion, frustration and impotence. How did one understand a situation that had never been explained, created by a man who was now dead?

Cole straightened, shrugged and reached for the bottle of wine to top up their glasses. He lifted his eyes and she saw that they were as hard as agates. He'd emotionally retreated behind an impenetrable shield. 'So, I got an interesting email today. A client of mine is having a garden party at his sixteenth-century chateau in Burgundy next weekend to celebrate Bastille Day and I'm invited.'

She blinked, not sure she'd heard him correctly. They'd been having an intense conversation about his brother and now he was talking about a garden party in France?

What?

'Why don't you come with me?' he asked.

Okay, had she stepped into a strange metaverse? He was acting as if they hadn't just had a deep conversation about his past and his family, and she wondered how he could switch subjects so quickly. 'We were talking about your brother, Cole,' she pointed out.

His shrug was annoyingly nonchalant. 'Now we're not. So, will you come? We can fly from Burgundy to London, and you can see where I live. I might be able to fly back with you on Tuesday, depending on my schedule.'

She stared at him, expecting to see another head emerging. 'I can't go to France, then London, with you.'

Cole lifted his glass and sipped. 'Why not? Your sisters will only be back the following Saturday so it's not like you have to be back for them.'

It was the craziest idea she'd ever heard. She couldn't just fly off on a whim. It wasn't what she did, who she was. She wasn't the girl who jetted off on private planes to attend garden parties at French chateaux. She worked, she studied, she looked after Nixi and Snow—she didn't *jet*.

'And, you know, even if your younger sisters were due home, why couldn't you take that time for yourself?'

She jerked up, her spine steel-rod straight. 'Because that's my job—that's what I agreed to do.'

'When you and Addi worked out your division of

duties, was there a clause that said you couldn't do anything for yourself any more, that you couldn't do anything fun?' Cole challenged her. 'I'm not asking you to marry me, Lex, I'm asking you to come to a weekend party with me, to visit my home.'

He was moving the goalposts and she didn't like it. They were supposed to be having a road-trip fling. It wasn't supposed to last beyond this time in Rhodes. And, damn it, she was also mad because she was so tempted to say yes, to run away, to feel young, impulsive and free again. But she was terrified that, if she did, she'd never be content to return to the life she knew, the life she'd carefully created to give her sisters the stability she'd never had.

'You can't keep putting your life on hold for your sisters, Lex.'

'Why not? Why can't I do exactly that?' she demanded, her voice rising. And how dare he say that? He hadn't walked in her shoes. He didn't know what motivated her to make the choices she had.

'You're putting them first because nobody put you first, Lex. You're making sure that their lives are as wonderful as you can make them because nobody did that for you.'

Oh! He was right and she hated him for saying what she barely could admit to herself. She was trying to be all and do all for Nixi and Snow to make the little girl who still lived deep inside her feel better about herself, to feel worthy.

'It's not fair on you.'

Fair? Ah, now there was a statement she could

fight. 'You have to be kidding me! You, of all people, know that life isn't fair. I learned that early and I learned that hard! And I did it without the cushion of money. How dare you criticise what I do, the choices I've made?'

'I wasn't criticising, I just want you to—'

'Stop talking!' Lex shouted.

She couldn't hear any more, take any more. She felt emotionally battered, not necessarily by Cole but by the old emotions, hurts and truths he'd pulled to the surface. She didn't take time for herself, and had put her life on hold, possibly because she still believed she needed to prove she was worthy of love.

She needed air, she needed space and she desperately needed to be alone.

Lex held up her hands and backed away. 'This was just supposed to be about sex, Cole. Why are we shouting at each other?'

'I'm not the one shouting,' he pointed out, his tone ultra-reasonable. 'And I thought we agreed that we could be friends as well as lovers.'

She held his eyes, her eyes cool. 'One question, Cole.'

He arched one eyebrow, waiting.

'Was deflecting me off the subject of your brother worth this argument?' When he didn't answer her, she spoke again, her voice as brittle as frost-eaten winter grass. 'I'll leave you alone to think about that.'

Lex grabbed a torch from the kitchen drawer and walked to the main building and back, kicking her way through the snow. By the time she returned, she was miserable, freezing and had a pulsing headache. Knowing that she had some pain killers in her bag, she slipped into the master suite, found her bag and the pills, swallowed them down and sat down on the edge of the bed. Would Cole sleep here with her tonight? Would they spend the rest of the trip in silence? Would he simply ignore her, deciding that she wasn't worth his time and energy? Joelle had been the master of the silent treatment and had had a doctorate in making her feel as if she wasn't worth her time and attention after one of their many clashes.

Lex heard his footsteps but didn't look up. He sat down on the bed beside her and his arm snaked around her waist.

'Are you still mad?' Cole murmured in her ear, placing his mouth on the bare skin below her ear.

Yes. No. She was still furious, but more at herself than at him. He'd sliced away the half-truths she'd told herself, and she hadn't liked what she'd seen. She'd been so convinced that she'd recovered from the wounds her mother had inflicted, but she hadn't done as much healing as she'd thought, and she hated that. Hated that the past still had such a hold over her.

She shrugged and couldn't stop herself from leaning into him, soaking up some of his strength. He felt like a barrier between her and the world. At this moment, whatever wanted to hurt her had to come through him.

Lex gave herself a mental shake, telling herself to see things as they were, not as she wanted them to be.

They were short-term lovers, as he'd said—friends. It wasn't his job to protect her.

This was all so confusing.

It shouldn't be. He was just a fling, not someone who would be in her life long-term. She had no intention of allowing someone into her heart only to watch them walk away a few weeks or months later, dunking her in a vat of hurt and disappointment. Cole would never be able to put her, and what she needed, first.

Lex ran her hands up and down her face. 'I don't know,' she answered him honestly.

'Fair enough,' he replied, before standing and scooping her up to hold her against his chest.

'What are you doing?' she demanded, wide-eyed.

'Taking you to bed and, after I've made you feel boneless, you're going to take a nap before we eat.'

'I never nap,' Lex told him.

Cole swiped his lips across her mouth. 'You will,' he promised her as he walked her to her side of the bed and lowered her down. 'I'm sorry if what I said pushed your buttons.'

Lex noticed that he hadn't apologised for what he'd said. Why should he, since he was right?

'If I agree with that, will you admit that you changed the subject to avoid speaking about your brother?'

He nodded. 'Yes. I didn't want to talk about him any more, but I still do want you to come to France with me.'

'I thought this would end when we got back to Cape Town.'

'I'm still not promising you anything, Lex, but neither do I think we need to discard each other like last night's takeaways. We're enjoying each other, let's keep doing that.'

She started to shake her head, to tell him she couldn't, that it was impossible, but pulled the words back at the last minute. She was reacting out of habit, because doing something fun wasn't what she did, wasn't something she thought she deserved. She could go to France. Nothing was keeping her here. It was the opportunity of a lifetime. She'd never travelled out of the country and didn't know when she'd next have the chance to use her unstamped passport. Excitement bubbled beneath her skin, skipped into her blood and coursed through her body.

It had been so long since she'd felt excited that she almost didn't recognise the emotion. But because she was cautious, because a little voice deep inside was screaming at her not to make any impulsive decisions, she lifted her hand to his jaw and told him she'd think about it.

'Good enough.' Cole lay down next to her and pulled the band from her hair, combing his fingers through her bright strands. He stroked his thumb down the cord in her neck and she looked into his warm eyes. 'Can I just say a few more things?'

Lex tensed, wishing he wouldn't. She'd heard enough and had too many thoughts careering around her head. She just wanted to feel.

'Although I do think you neglect yourself, I'm also in awe of you, Lex. I think you are amazing, and I have the greatest respect for you. You are raising your sisters, working, studying, juggling more than a couple of balls in the air and not letting any of them fall.'

Tension seeped out of her body. 'You juggle dozens of balls too.'

'No, sweetheart, my balls are money-related—work. If I drop a ball, I lose money, not a big deal. If you drop a ball, your sisters could be affected, your degree and your second income. Money is easy, people are difficult—complicated. The stakes don't compare.'

Warmth seeped into her eyes and her hand came up to touch his hair, her fingers stroking his scalp. That was the nicest thing she'd heard him, or anyone, say. And she didn't know how much she needed to hear the words until he'd said them.

She felt recognised and seen. Understood. And how strange was it that it was this solitary man, someone so different from her in life experiences, who made her feel affirmed. She'd had so little emotional support, so few people cheering her on, that a part of her wanted to ask him to repeat himself so that she could roll around in the sunshine of his words.

'Thank you for saying that.'

'But you can be pretty scary and damn bossy when you're mad.'

She heard the teasing note in his voice and laughed. How could she go from blisteringly angry to laughter so quickly? Did the 'why' even matter? He was here with her and they were talking—friends again. And lovers.

Talking about loving… Lex used her core muscles to launch herself upwards, her mouth seeking his, her kiss full of thanks, gratitude and a huge hit of want and need.

'I think you should take my clothes off,' Lex instructed, her voice growly with need.

Because he wasn't a saint, and because making love to her was what he most wanted to do, Cole decided that was a fine idea indeed.

'You have the prettiest body,' he told her, pulling her jersey up her ribcage, exposing her pale and lovely skin to his hot gaze. Her bra was plain white, functional rather than pretty, and the thought that he wanted to see her in jewel colours—reds, violets and deep greens—flitted through his mind as he placed his mouth on her nipple and sucked her, fabric and all, into his mouth.

Lex responded to his deep kiss by moaning and trying to wrap her hand around his erection, hampered by the material of his jeans. Holding herself in a half-sit-up position, she pulled his earlobe into her mouth and nibbled on it, sending a warm, fast burst of electricity along every nerve ending he possessed.

'So you like me when I'm bossy, right?' Lex asked, his tone teasing.

'In certain circumstances,' he replied. 'For instance, if you told me to get naked, then I'd listen.'

He saw green fire in Lex's eyes through her half-closed lids. 'Get naked, Cole,' she ordered him.

Eager to play this game, Cole pulled away from her, stood next to the bed and pulled off his jersey, slowly. She beckoned him closer and, kneeling on the bed as he stood, placed her mouth on his sternum, her tongue coming out to touch his hot skin. Cole closed his eyes, his clothes falling to the floor as Lex's clever mouth drifted down across the hard muscles of his stomach, and lower, to where the band of his jeans rested.

He reached down to undo his trousers but Lex smacked his hands away. 'My job,' she told him, her tone suggesting that he not disagree.

He pulled his hands away and their eyes connected as she undid the buttons holding his jeans together.

She looked up at him and Cole's heart flipped over backwards. Damn, she had no idea how sexy she was. He looked down into those eyes that were the exact colour of the nephrite jade Buddha figure he'd bought at auction last year. They were shockingly deep and, like the statue, Lex was rare, special and pretty damn amazing. She was bright, compelling, courageous and massively strong-willed, stronger than she realised and tougher than she gave herself credit for.

He was in awe of her...

In another life, if he'd been another guy, he'd find a way to keep her in his life.

But that was impossible. He couldn't give her anything more than sex. Their time together was limited. She was raising a family and he was terrible at relationships. He always messed them up by pulling away, by sabotaging them.

But this was the first woman to tempt him into those turbulent waters in over a decade. He had to resist her, had to resist the idea of them. The lines between lust and like were blurring.

Slow down, idiot. Right now. Because, if you don't, you're going to come out of this bloody and bruised.

Lex pushed her hands between his skin and the fabric of his underwear and jeans and tugged everything down. He shed his clothes and, when she reached for him, he shook his head. If she touched him with her lips, if she sucked him, this would all be over very fast indeed. No, he needed to wring pleasure out of every moment they had together.

'My turn to be bossy,' Cole told her, tugging her to her feet. As she stood on the bed in front of him, he stripped her quickly, throwing her clothes to the floor. When she was gloriously naked, he placed feather-light kisses on her ribcage, nibbled her collarbone and dragged his tongue across that sweet spot between her neck and ear. Lex picked up his hand and placed it on her breast, but he wouldn't be rushed. This was his time, so he tickled and teased, tasting her skin on the back of her knee, the arch of her foot. He nuzzled the special space between her thighs, but after a few seconds pulled away to nibble her hip bone, to taste her belly button, to suck on her breasts.

And when Lex's demands became insistent, when her moans deepened, he pulled back and started to explore her lovely body all over again. When she thumped his shoulder with her small fist, when her eyes turned stormy with passion, liquid with need, he placed his mouth on her. That small contact made her orgasm and, wanting her to get off again, he slid two fingers into her and nuzzled her to another high.

Pliant, out of breath and loose with pleasure, she rolled over onto her stomach and lifted her hips, seeming to know what he wanted, how he needed her. He reached for the condom he'd tossed onto the bed earlier, rolled it on and, after widening her knees, slid into her slick warmth and closed his eyes. *Home*, he thought.

He didn't have time to interrogate that thought because he felt Lex push back against him and he recognised the tension in her body. She wanted to come again, and he was fully prepared to take it slow, to make her burn. But Lex had other plans...

Suddenly she was rocking, he was pumping and he heard Lex's scream of pleasure echoing down a tunnel. Her inner walls tightened around him and a stream of pure energy rocketed through him, spinning him away.

Amazing, Cole thought. He tightened his arm around her waist, anchoring her to him, his big body covering hers. They couldn't have a future, but they had this.

And this was pretty astounding.

CHAPTER ELEVEN

ON SUNDAY, JUST over a week after they'd arrived at Rossdale, the weather cleared and they could make their way down the mountain, this time with Cole behind the wheel. Snow still covered the hills but the road was finally navigable. Lex kept her eyes on her side mirror until the ski-lodge disappeared from sight. For as long as she lived, she'd always remember these magical days she spent snowbound with Cole. The ski resort would always hold a magical place in her heart.

She'd never return to this place but she would always remember making love in front of the fire, spending the afternoon wrapped up in a cashmere blanket in Cole's arms and drinking red wine as she watched the snow drift to the ground. Sharing his shower, waking up to him nuzzling her breast with his stubbled cheek and his hand between her legs would be X-rated memories she'd savour.

Returning to her sister-focused life was going to be a lot tougher than she'd bargained for.

Despite knowing their affair had an expiration date, despite constantly reminding herself this was a brief fling and that he wasn't interested in any type of commitment, she couldn't stop herself from wanting more. She might, because she was a complete moron, just want everything.

Him. For ever.

Lex looked out of the window, feeling the burn of tears in the back of her throat. She didn't know if she was emotional because time was running out or because she was angry at not being able to control her emotions and expectations, to keep her heart in check.

Both, probably.

Cole steered the SUV around the last steep corner and they moved from a dirt road to one covered in tarmac. There were clumps of snow on the grass and a number of trees were buckled and bent from the wind and the weight of the snow. The storm had been unexpected and impressive.

Words that perfectly described Cole.

Cole reached across the console and slid his hand over hers, lifting her knuckles to his mouth and kissing her skin. He darted her a quick look. 'I had the best time with you, Lex. It was a marvellous break.'

For her too. And, despite trying not to let her imagination run riot, she could see them doing it again. And again. Sneaking away for a week here, a few days there to be on their own—him running away from his work, her from her studies and the girls. Without any effort at all, she could see them taking family holidays, with Cole teaching her sisters, and later their own kids, to ski and snowboard.

Instead of being blurry, that mental snapshot was

crystal-clear. A dark-haired son and a red-headed daughter, or any combination of sex and colouring. He was the only person she could imagine having a child with, being with, committing to.

The only man she would, could, fall in love with. No, that was wrong. She already loved him. And, damn, how inconvenient and insane was *that*?

She couldn't handle the implications of her rogue thought and pushed it away, hoping that the feeling would fade. She needed to think of something else, *anything* else.

'Did you get an email back from your brother explaining about Charlie?' Lex asked, thinking about the constant references to Charlie at the lodge.

Cole shook his head. 'No. I don't really expect to. My brother has never been good at giving me what I need.'

After their argument, they'd both avoided the subject of her family and his, choosing instead to get to know each other better, talking about the things new lovers did—art, music, travels and politics. Cole had done some work. She'd found a book to read in the library. He'd skied and she'd tried to. They'd made love.

A lot.

'In some ways, I'm angrier with Sam than I am with my father. Sam could've defied Grenville, he could've chosen to have a relationship with me, but he didn't,' Cole explained, and Lex heard the bitterness in his voice.

'You're assuming that Sam is as strong as you, Cole.'

'What do you mean?'

'I don't think you realise how strong you are. It took enormous guts, determination and self-belief to achieve what you have with no help or emotional support from your family. Maybe Sam simply wasn't good at conflict, or too weak to buck your father's wishes. Maybe he feels intense guilt that he wasn't there for you more.'

'Doubt that,' Cole muttered.

Lex felt a wave of gratitude for having her sisters in her life, particularly Addi. She'd had Addi to steady her, to give her love and support, but Cole lived his life solo.

'Have you decided whether you are coming to France with me or not?' Cole asked, placing her hand on his thigh and holding it down.

Lex looked away and bit her lip. She'd thought that agreeing to accompany him to Rhodes was brave but flying to Europe would be way out of her comfort zone. He was giving her the opportunity to explore another country, and one of the greatest cities in the world. When would she have that chance again? She should say yes on that basis alone.

Honestly, there wasn't a decent reason for her to say no. The girls were still away and Addi would be the first to tell her to take the opportunity, and that she deserved to take some time for herself.

Because she'd experienced massive unpredictability as a child, and wanted a stable life for her sisters and for herself, she'd made a religion of being rigid, of putting her sisters' needs before hers. She was so scared of letting them down—thinking that, in never allowing them to feel insecure and disappointed, she'd heal the wounds her mother and childhood had inflicted on her—that she never allowed any unpredictability to creep into her life.

But life was unpredictable and the ability to deal with change made people resilient and stronger. She wasn't doing the girls, and herself, any favours by being so protective of their hearts and feelings. She wanted Nixi and Snow to live, to gulp down life, but to do that they had to have an example to follow. From Addi they were learning a solid work ethic. Maybe she could teach them to be brave.

She could go with him or spend the weekend in her house binge watching box sets. That sounded so... sad. She didn't want to live a small, sad life any more.

She took a deep breath. 'I'd like to, thank you.'

'Great. Do you have a passport?'

She had a UK passport so there would be no visa issues, which she told him.

Cole squeezed her hand. 'That makes it easier.' He thought for a moment before speaking. 'I need to fly to Mauritius to look at some assets and businesses.'

Seriously, how many businesses did Thorpe Industries own?

'Okay, then I'll arrange for my jet to meet us when we reach Bloemfontein. And, if I leave Cape Town tonight and hit the ground running first thing in the morning, I should be able to complete my business in four days and fly back Thursday morning. We could fly out Thursday evening, spend Friday in Paris and head for Burgundy on Saturday morning.'

He was offering to show her Paris as well. *Oh, wow.* 'Won't you be tired of flying?' she asked.

'Honey, I'm not the one flying the plane,' he pointed out, amused, and laughed when she blushed. 'And I employ two flight crews because I'm always in the air.

'Would taking an extra-long weekend work for you?' he asked.

Uh...yes.

Cole grinned when she gave him her answer and she thought how much younger he looked when his smile hit his eyes, when he looked truly happy.

As for her, Lex felt as though he'd lifted her and swung her around, setting her back on her feet when she was off-balance and giddy. She was going to Paris. She could talk French and test her proficiency in the language. She could see the Eiffel Tower and visit the Louvre. Then she'd hop over to London. She felt breathless, as if her heart was trying to escape, and adrenalin coursed through her system.

Best of all, she'd be with Cole.

But underneath the excitement...oh, so faint but still there...lurked fear, warning her not to become too excited because there was always a chance that he'd disappoint her. Because that was what people did, what she'd experienced over and over again.

But sometimes they didn't. Sometimes people did what they said they would. Cole was too straightforward and too in-your-face honest to play games, to mess with her emotions.

She was going to Europe, and she was allowed to feel excited and thrilled about her first overseas visit.

And about spending more time with Cole.

'You are going to have such a wonderful time and I'm so happy for you, Lex.'

Addi placed her hands on Lex's shoulders and Lex looked at their reflections, so different. For the first time in for ever she didn't compare herself to her gorgeous sister. She looked…well, pretty damn amazing herself.

Earlier in the week, Cole had called and told her he'd managed to complete his business early and that they could fly out mid-Thursday morning if she could meet him at the airport. He'd made a late-night reservation at Mathieu, a three-Michelin-star restaurant on the Boulevard St-Germain. She'd looked up the restaurant online, and it was fancy with a capital F.

Panicking because she had nothing to wear to an exclusive Michelin-star restaurant, or a garden party at a French chateau, she'd called Addi, who'd immediately flown into action.

In a second-hand clothing store off Adderley Street, they found all she needed. She was now the proud owner of a designer little black dress she'd wear to Mathieu tonight, and a couple of classic dresses that were suitable for the French countryside. She was travelling in a long pink pleated skirt with a fitted turtleneck in the same colour. *Pink*—it was a colour she never wore because everyone knew that redheads couldn't wear pink. Or red. Or orange.

Her outfit wasn't blush-pink, or salmon-pink—
no, it was flaming pink, a hot pink, the colour of
printed sunsets on tourist T-shirts. It was a pink that
screamed *look at me!* and stamped its foot if you
didn't. To someone who routinely wore black, this
shade was a shock to her senses.

But, damn, it looked good on her.

She looked stunning, like herself but not. Bella—
a stylist Addi knew from who knew where—had arrived early and spent a long time making her curls
straight, then used a flat iron on them until her hair
fell past her shoulders. Then she pulled her hair back
into a tight, sleek tail, wrapping strands over one another to conceal the band.

Addi watched, fascinated, as she placed a light
foundation over her face, evening out the colour of
her freckles but not hiding them. Bella showed her
how to apply smoky eye-shadow and painted her lips
with a natural-coloured lipstick she assured her would
last all day.

'You look sophisticated and lovely,' Addi told her.
She picked up her phone and snapped a couple of pic-
tures. 'These are going on the family message group.
The girls will be beside themselves.'

Addi and Bella left, and Lex closed her suitcase
and checked, yet again, that she had everything she
needed. She picked up her case and looked at her re-
flection in the freestanding mirror, cocking her head
to the side. She could see this person with Cole in
his usual, rich-as-Croesus life. She looked sophisticated and successful, cool and competent. Classy.

She didn't look like a curly-haired chauffeur, a harried young woman raising two little girls or a part-time student. She looked like someone had waved a wand and made her...chic.

When Joelle had got her to change her looks, she'd gone to extreme lengths and had continued bleaching her hair and wearing thick make-up. Then, since she'd embraced her natural look, she'd never worn anything but a little mascara and lip gloss. Maybe she could find some middle ground. Straightening her hair every day would be impossible, but maybe she could start wearing tinted moisturiser, a little eyeshadow and this gorgeous shade of lipstick.

As for her clothes, while she wasn't a 'dress up and look smart' kind of girl, maybe she could start wearing something other than black jeans, long-sleeved T-shirts and vintage jackets. She should start introducing a little more colour and variety into her life. She was allowed to experiment with her looks, to dress up or down, to wear make-up or not. She was allowed to swap things around, try something new. It wasn't as if she was hiding behind a thick foundation and bright-blonde hair any more.

She could change her looks without changing herself.

Lex grinned. She was having a bit of a Cinderella moment, but instead of going to the ball in a carriage she'd be flying on a private plane and going to a garden party.

As if she'd summoned him, the doorbell chimed downstairs. Her driver was here.

She slung her bag over her shoulder and grabbed the handle. Her smile split her face as excitement danced up and down her spine.

Lex was about to embark on her truly excellent adventure.

Mr Thorpe, your brother requests your presence in Thailand. He has received special dispensation from the head monk to meet with you Saturday afternoon. He needs to tell you about Charlie. If you miss this opportunity, he does not know when, if ever, he will be able to meet with you again.

Sitting in his car outside Lex's cottage, Cole looked at the email from Sam's lawyer again and cursed. He'd received it as he touched down in Cape Town just an hour ago, earlier than he'd expected. The email was brief, but it felt as if every word was imbued with urgency. So Sam knew who this Charlie was and now felt the need to share the knowledge with him.

Good of him.

Cole was tempted to blow off his brother's request and whisk Lex off to Paris as he'd planned. Man, he'd missed her. He'd missed her laughter, the way she turned to him in her sleep and draped her thigh over his and placed her hand on his heart. He missed her clothes next to his in the wardrobe, the smell of her hair, the way she looked at him, her deep-green eyes glinting with affection and desire.

And he missed the sex. He really missed making love to her.

But if he didn't go to Thailand, if he ignored Sam's request, he'd never know who Charlie was and he knew, somewhere deep down, that whatever Sam had to tell him would fill in many of the blanks, would give him the answers he'd always sought.

He glanced at Lex's cottage, frowning as he tried to work out how to make this work.

He could change their plans, take her to Thailand and leave her on a beach while he visited his brother. But he knew that afterwards he would tell her what had happened between Sam and him, how he felt and what emotions he was experiencing. She'd hold his hand, lean her head on his shoulder and he wouldn't feel so alone.

If she did that, he'd pull the cork from the damn dyke and all his emotions would flood out and drown him. He'd say way more than he should—that he adored her, that he couldn't bear the thought of leaving Cape Town and her behind, that he wanted them to...

What? Have a long-distance relationship? Be his lover? Be his significant other, his girlfriend, his wife...his *something*?

Practically, realistically, they had too many obstacles to overcome. He only needed to visit Cape Town and Port Louis, the capital city of Mauritius, once, maybe twice, more before he'd manage to rid himself of all Thorpe Industries assets and businesses. He could see Lex then, but after those two brief trips he wouldn't be returning to Africa any time soon. He'd been giving his hedge fund and his venture capital business minimal time lately. He'd employed analysts to help him with his workload but he needed to take full control again. He missed his real work, the adrenalin of making massive stock buys, finding new companies to invest in and grow.

And then there was the issue of her sisters. Lex was raising two little girls and it would be disingenuous to suggest that her being the equivalent of a single mum wasn't a factor. If they were together, he'd have to share her time, attention and energy with her younger sisters, and at the very least be a role model to them. He couldn't see himself sharing Lex and living in a noisy house with two young girls when he was so very used to being on his own in his tidy and quiet house.

He'd never had a father, or much of an older brother, so how could he be either to her sisters?

Another obstacle was that Lex's life was here, in Cape Town. And, while he had all the money in the world to pay for her to fly to see him, or he to see her, he knew that a long-distance relationship, seeing each other occasionally, wasn't something she'd contemplate. And wouldn't having little bites of time with her—a weekend here, a week there—make the times they spent apart harder to endure?

Cole sighed, knowing that he'd exhausted the practicalities and had to get down to the nitty-gritty of what was keeping him from forming a solid attachment to Lex.

Just get on with it, Thorpe, you've played this song before.

A core truth was that he'd made connections with women before and thought he'd met someone special. He'd tiptoe into a relationship but within a few weeks, sometimes a couple of months, he'd always end up feeling trapped, desperate to run.

Right now, he was besotted with Lex, couldn't touch her enough, wanted to make love to her constantly, hated being away from her, felt the need to be near her, talking to her, and having her fall asleep in his arms. He could see her rounded with his child, having a house filled with two little girls and their children running around, loud, messy and full of laughter and love. A house and life that would be the antithesis of his cold and lonely childhood.

But he'd had dreams before—though not this bright and vivid—and knew that feeling like this never lasted. In a month or two—maybe longer, because Lex entranced him like no other woman had before—he'd cool down, pull away. She'd have questions and he wouldn't be able to explain why he felt the need to run.

In his twenties, he'd put his failed relationships down to choosing the wrong woman, timing and mistaking sex for love. Now that he was older, he knew he was the problem, because he wanted something they couldn't give.

And he was doing it again.

Because no matter how much he adored her, how close he came to falling in love with her, she could never give him enough or what he really wanted—

love and acceptance. No, that was wrong. She couldn't give him his father's love and acceptance.

Grenville was dead and, no matter how many times he told himself that he was an idiot for wanting something impossible or unachievable, it didn't stop his heart from yearning for it.

And, maybe, he thought that if he hadn't been worthy of Grenville's love then he wasn't worthy of anyone's love and couldn't trust it when he was offered it. Consciously or subconsciously, he might even have decided that, not having been able to interact with his father or have his love, then he'd *become* Grenville—cold, unemotional and soulless—to protect himself against future hurts.

It all sounded a bit weird, a lot crazy, but the truth was that his relationship, or non-relationship, with his father had affected and coloured his relationships with women. It would do the same with Lex.

He had an unhealed wound but that didn't mean that he should create wounds in other people's souls.

No, it was better to walk away now, while their feelings could be harnessed, corralled. It would hurt a little, more than likely a lot, but he was trying to protect her, trying to do the right thing.

That had to count for something, hadn't it? Then why couldn't he make his hand reach for the door and get his body to leave the car?

CHAPTER TWELVE

THE MOMENT SHE wrenched open her front door and saw Cole's hard face, Lex knew she wasn't going to Paris.

Or anywhere.

Despite her heart dropping to her toes, she couldn't help thinking that he looked amazing, taking in his black suit trousers and light-grey jacket, which he wore over a V-necked pale-green jersey. He hadn't shaved for a couple of days and his beard was at the length she loved most, long enough to feel soft, short enough still to be considered stubble.

Lex fought the impulse to throw herself into his arms, to stand on her toes and lift her mouth to his, but his remote expression had her holding back, her hand still on the knob of her front door. She stepped back and gestured for him to come inside, hearing her thunderous heartbeat in her ears.

Please don't disappoint me, Cole. Please don't say the words hovering on your lips.

'Come on in,' she invited.

Cole stepped into the tiny hallway and she saw

the heat in his eyes as he took in her bright outfit and her straight hair. He opened his mouth to say something. Was he about to compliment her? Did he like the way she looked? But then he snapped it closed. He jammed his hands into the pockets of his trousers and rocked on his heels.

Right, so he wasn't going to kiss her. Not a good sign.

'Are you okay?' she asked, folding her arms and digging the tips of her shaking fingers into her ribs.

Cole rubbed a hand over his lower jaw. 'Just tired. It's been a long week.'

She waited for him to elaborate, but he looked away from her to examine the many photographs hanging on the wall. The biggest one, dead centre, was a photograph of the five sisters laughing. She couldn't remember when it had been taken, or by whom, but it captured all the love they shared, the enjoyment they had in each other's company. Cole looked at that photograph for a long time before shaking his head and closing his eyes.

Tired of waiting for him to speak, and needing an explanation before she exploded, Lex spoke. 'The weekend is off, isn't it? You're cancelling on me, aren't you?'

He met her eyes. His were a muddy brown instead of their normal topaz, and eventually he nodded. 'Yes.'

She'd expected his answer, had braced herself for it, yet she was still shocked when he confirmed what she suspected. 'Is there a reason?' she asked, forcing the words through her teeth.

Out of the corner of her eye, she saw Addi coming down the stairs and waved her away. This was between Cole and her.

'I need to go to Thailand,' he told her.

Pulling words out of him was like pulling dinosaur teeth out of stone. Where was the laughing man who'd beaten her at Scrabble, the warm-eyed guy who'd brought her hot coffee and kissed her shoulder and neck as she'd waited for the caffeine to kick in? Where had he gone?

'Okay, so I'll come with you to Thailand.' Overseas was overseas, after all.

'Sorry, no.'

Ah, so Cole didn't want her going anywhere with him. Message received.

Her lips pressed together so tightly, she didn't think any blood could reach them and her shoulders were close to her ears. She could visualise her heart shrinking, becoming smaller with each breath she took, and a cold hand held her stomach in a vice-like grip.

Oh, hello disappointment, my old friend. You haven't changed at all.

But she had. She wasn't the timid little girl who'd taken life's punches on the chin, who'd fallen down and then scuttled away. She was stronger, better, older, damn it. Anger, hot and wild, coursed through her system and Lex felt the pressure build up in her head. His behaviour wasn't acceptable. Not now. Not ever.

Don't yell, Lex.

As she knew from Joelle, losing one's temper lessened the impact of the message.

Lex dropped her arms and jabbed a finger into Cole's chest. 'You asked me to go to France with you, you told me to step out of my comfort zone and you encouraged me to be adventurous,' Lex reminded him, her voice sounding brittle. Tears had started to gather in her throat, but she'd be damned if she'd let him see them. He didn't deserve anything but cold fury.

'We've spent the past few days exchanging text messages about what we'd do in Paris, in London, how you wanted to take me wine-tasting in the Pouilly-Fuissé region. Give me a reason for blowing me off, Cole, when I took the huge leap of trusting you, of stepping outside my comfort zone.'

Whatever his reason for cancelling the trip, it was more important than her. She wasn't, in any way, his priority.

'I told you that I've been disappointed by many people in many ways, but I never expected yours to be a name I added to that list.'

Lex didn't drop her eyes from his, and she clocked his regret, but couldn't ignore his determined expression. There would be no talking him out of this, no room for manoeuvre.

It was over. They were done.

All that was left was to say the words and make it official.

Lex's belly twisted into a complicated knot and she

felt as if she couldn't pull enough air into her lungs. Another person she loved and adored was about to walk away from her again. Really, she should be used to it by now.

For the first time ever, he didn't know what to say, how to end this. He knew he should tell her that they had no future, but he couldn't make his tongue form the words. 'Lex... I...'

She met his eyes and within those fathomless green depths he saw pain, but also pride. 'You don't need to strain yourself to find the right words, Cole.'

How could he tell her, in the nicest way possible, that this was about him and not her? 'I really do have to go to Thailand,' he told her, wondering if he should just bite the bullet and tell her that he was going to see Sam.

No, he needed to do this alone, to handle this himself. He'd been dealing with the fallout from his family on his own his entire life. If this was the last time he would speak to his brother, and it sounded as if it might be, then he wanted to finish as he'd started— by himself.

Besides, if he let Lex into his thoughts and heart again, he might not have the courage to let her go when they returned. Until he sabotaged their relationship down the line, when he would hurt her far more than he would now.

Admittedly, judging by the pain in her eyes, he was currently doing a great job.

He wanted to howl and beat his fists, but Lex

looked dignified and aloof. She glanced at her front door, a silent gesture for him to leave, but he didn't know if he could. Doubt washed over him and he found himself backtracking. 'I need to return in about six weeks.'

She nodded enthusiastically, faking her excitement. 'Yes, sure, of course, I'll meet up with you again! I'll just come running when you call, okay?' she retorted, sarcastic condemnation in her voice.

'Why would I ever give you another chance to disappoint me again, Cole? Another chance to make promises and plans which you'll break with a flimsy excuse?' she demanded. 'Do you really expect me to fall back into line, thrilled to be in the sexy billionaire's bed again?'

Disdain coated her words and Cole felt two feet tall.

'I can't figure out a way for it to work, Lex,' he told her, sounding a little desperate.

'Of course it can't work, Cole, because I would be expected to do all the work. For us to keep seeing each other, I'd have to agree to wait around for you until you could return to Cape Town for a flying visit or until I could carve out time away from work, my studies and the girls.' Her expression was a curious combination of sadness and ferocity. 'And that's assuming that you can make a commitment to me, which I don't think you can. Or even want to.'

He could, *today*. He just didn't know how he'd feel in three months, in six. Would he still be crazy about her, or would he be looking for the nearest exit?

She fiddled with the hem of her jacket. 'Look, even if we decided to try the long-distance thing, I'd quickly run out of patience with that sort of set-up,' she told him. 'I am aware that my circumstances are challenging, that I have more responsibilities than the average woman in her late twenties. But the thing is, Cole, after dealing with a couple of hard knocks I have this crazy notion that I deserve some happy.'

'Of course you do,' he agreed.

'When the time comes for Nixi and Snow to date, I want to teach them not to settle for just anyone, that they are worthy of being more than an option, that they need to insist on being a choice. And I've got to practise what I preach. I need to be your *choice*. I won't be an option.'

She was asking for more than he could give her. 'I'm not good at long-term relationships, Lex.'

'So you say, Cole.' She shrugged, trying for casualness but missing it by a mile. 'But I'm prepared to wait for someone who is, someone who can give me everything I need: love, emotional security, to put me and my needs first. To be his priority. If that guy isn't you, and it obviously isn't, then I'll wait.'

His entire body rebelled at the idea of her with someone else. It felt as though an earthquake were rolling through him. He couldn't give her what she needed but letting her leave his life was harder than he'd thought.

'I think we are done here,' Lex gestured for him to leave. In a fog of confusion and regret, of hurt and relief, Cole walked onto her front step and turned to face her. She looked remote but impossibly lovely.

'I really hope you find happiness, Cole.'

He nodded, wondering how he'd ever manage to do that without her in his life. There was nothing he could say. He felt numb.

He swallowed and forced his tongue to form a series of words. 'I still think you're pretty amazing, Lex.'

'I know you do. You like me and you want me, but you don't trust yourself to love me the way I love you.'

What?

'You love me?' he croaked.

She held his eyes and nodded. 'Yes, of course I do. I love you enough to let you go and I love myself enough to demand more.'

Lex turned away and stepped back, closing the door in his face. He bit his lip to stop himself from calling out to her, from pounding on her door, and forced his feet to head in the direction of his car. He couldn't trust himself, couldn't take the chance...

Couldn't hurt her more than he was already doing.

Lex was out of his life, just as he'd planned.

He never thought that losing her would hurt this much.

Lex and Addi sat at a wooden table overlooking the quaint fishing harbour of Hout Bay, newspaper-wrapped fish and chips in front of them. Addi's iced tea was half-finished and Lex hadn't touched hers. Neither had she managed to lift any food to her mouth.

She could cope intellectually with the notion of Cole not wanting a relationship with her, and accepted that tears were part of her immediate future, although hopefully she'd be done crying by the time the girls returned in a week. But she strongly objected to losing her appetite.

That was a step too far.

Addi broke off a piece of fish, lifted it to her mouth and groaned. 'Man, this is still the best place to eat fresh fish.'

'If you say so,' Lex replied, watching a fishing trawler trundle into port accompanied by a flock of squawking seagulls. The trawler's once-bright hull had faded to a washed-out blue and Lex sympathised. 'Washed out' was a perfect way to describe how she felt.

Not having Cole in her life—the man wasn't even in the country!—had sucked the colour from the world. Sounds felt muffled, everything she put in her mouth tasted like cardboard and her touch was either dulled or her nerve endings felt over-sensitised. And, because she was constantly blinking back tears, her eyesight wasn't operating in tip-top condition either. She was leaving out a sense and didn't have the mental energy to work out which it was.

'Have you heard from him?' Addi asked.

Lex stared at the fisherman who was wrestling a thick rope around a piling. 'No.'

'Nothing at all?' Addi demanded.

'We had an affair. It's over and done with.'

Addi dragged a chip through a pile of tomato sauce. 'Please tell me you used contraception, Lex.'

Lex glared at her. 'I think I learned that lesson from Joelle, Addi. I think we *all* learned that lesson.'

Addi nodded. 'Fair enough.' Addi popped a piece of fish into her mouth before speaking again. 'Jude Fisher offered me a job, with a huge pay rise.'

It took a couple of moments for her words to sink in, for them to make sense. If she understood Addi correctly, then they could stop worrying about money and how they were going to pay the bills when Cole sold off the hospitality sector of Thorpe Industries. Her heart might be broken but at least they didn't have to worry about how to feed, clothe and educate two growing girls.

Lex pulled up a smile. 'That's great, Ads, congratulations.'

Addi pushed her half-eaten portion of food away and twisted her silver ring round and round her finger. Despite having good news, she still looked worried and anxious. Nothing had ever been gained by avoiding a situation, so Lex gathered her courage, pushed her fist into her sternum and met Addi's eyes.

'What's wrong, Addison?'

'I'm just worried about you. I've never seen you so heartbroken.'

Lex wanted to object, to insist that she wasn't heartbroken, but the man she loved didn't love her so, yes, she supposed she was. It was horrible and heart-breaking knowing the person you wanted above everyone else didn't want you.

And, yes, she was having a rough time, but she sensed Addi's anxiety had nothing to do with her and her relationship with Cole. 'Addi...'

Addi's phone lit up with an incoming call, a number Lex didn't recognise, and Addi pounced on it, barking a curt greeting after lifting the device to her ear. Then she stood up and walked away from Lex to stand out of earshot, her lovely face taut with tension as she listened to whatever her caller was saying.

Her sister was keeping secrets, Lex decided, something they'd never done. They'd always shared everything, and knowing that Addi was shutting her out added another layer of hurt onto the ones Cole had painted on her soul.

So far, a broken heart hadn't killed her, but it hadn't made her stronger either. She felt sad, weak and emotionally helpless, mentally drained. But she had to hold herself together to keep her broken pieces from shattering. To keep moving.

She'd always been strong, always managed to keep going, to move forward. This time would be no different.

On Saturday afternoon, Cole sat on a remote beach close to the Cambodian border, sunglasses over his face. The air was hot and muggy and his thin cotton shirt stuck to his back. Hot and irritated, Cole pulled the fabric away from his skin and looked at his watch.

He caught the eye of the Thai waiter and lifted his

beer in a silent request for one more. The 'restaurant' where Sam had suggested they meet was no more than a mile from his monastery and comprised nothing more than an outdoor kitchen and two crudely built wooden benches and tables. But Cole was well-travelled enough to know that the best food was to be found in the unlikeliest of places. And, judging by the smell of garlic, chillies and lemongrass coming from somewhere behind him, someone was cooking an amazing fish curry.

Pity he'd lost the urge to eat since leaving Lex in Cape Town.

It was a stunning day, the sea glinting with shades of aqua and tanzanite blue, lazily rolling up the white sand beach. It was hard to believe that just days ago he'd been caught in a snowstorm and had experienced one of the Cape's wettest and wildest winters in history. The sky was a cobalt blue, practically perfect, yet Cole couldn't focus on the view, couldn't think of anything but that Lex should be here.

He'd missed her every second of every day since he'd pushed her away. He thought that he'd be fine, that his heart and soul would reshape themselves into what they'd been before they'd met her but...

No. They were still misshapen and anvil-heavy in his heart. He missed her with every breath he took, with every step he walked. His life no longer made sense without her in it.

Out of the corner of his eye, he caught the flash of an orange robe and he turned to see a tall, slim monk step onto the beach from the jungle, his bald head glinting white under the fierce sun. Cole watched as Sam walked towards him, noticing that his face was thinner and his cheekbones were pronounced.

The urge to walk away was strong. He didn't want to face his brother-that-never-was, but Cole couldn't let this go. He needed to speak to him, find some closure. He needed to repair the wound in his heart and maybe Sam, and his information, would help him do that.

Sam stopped a few metres from him and their eyes collided, so similar. He looked like his brother, like their father, but Cole doubted he'd ever acquire the serenity that he saw in Sam's eyes, nor the contentment.

Not unless he found a way back to Lex.

'Cole, you came,' Sam said, tipping his head to the side, a smile on his face.

Cole stood up and resisted the urge to wipe his damp hands on his thighs. 'Did you doubt that I would?'

Sam gave him a soft smile and sat down on the opposite side of the table. Right, so they weren't going to shake hands or hug. Good to know. He nodded at his beer. 'Want one?'

Sam didn't rise to the bait. 'I'll have a water, thanks.' Without waiting for Cole, he turned to the old man and greeted him in what sounded like remarkably fluent Thai. The old gent's face split into a wide smile. He looked beside himself with joy at the presence of a monk in his establishment. They spoke for a few minutes before the old man scuttled away to get his bottle of water.

Sam looked at Cole and raised his eyebrows. 'So, you found out about Charlie. How?'

'The ski-lodge in Rhodes. Everything carries the name—the pub, the ski runs, the company that owns it. It's the one part of Grenville's business that makes no sense, so I figure that this Charlie must be the reason that he hung on to such a loss-making asset. It's the only entity in Thorpe Industries that's raised questions. And the only one I can't sell.'

Sam looked puzzled. 'I thought you wanted the company. You spent enough money acquiring that block of Thorpe shares. I didn't want anything any more, so I thought it right to give it all to you.'

'I never wanted your damn money or shares, Sam! I wanted your attention, Dad's attention— Look, forget it!' Cole gripped the bridge of his nose in frustration. 'Just tell me who Charlie is, Sam. And, while you're at it, tell me why Grenville hated me so much.'

Sam took a long time to answer and with every second that ticked past Cole felt the tension rising. He braced himself to hear that their mum had had an affair and that she'd fallen pregnant by some man when she'd visited Rossdale. It was the only thing that made sense, that would explain why his father had hated him so. He didn't much care. If anything it would be a relief to know that he wasn't related to Grenville.

Eventually Sam spoke and, when he did, his eyes were dark with emotion. 'Charlie—Charlotte Jane— was our baby sister, Cole.'

* * *

I cannot believe that, after ten days of silence, he's texted me to collect him from the Vane!

Um...he owns Thorpe, and you're the company driver.

Sitting in the company SUV in a parking space next to the Vane's impressive entrance, Lex frowned at Addi's message and poked her tongue out at the screen. She hated it when her sister was super-logical, and hated it more when she was right.

Scrolling back, she stared down at the brief message from Cole, simply asking her to collect him at ten from the Vane.

When had he returned to Cape Town? How long was he staying? Could she afford to resign?

The last question was impossibly silly. Her job as the company driver was too good to give up and she'd continue doing it for as long as she could. But remaining professional while driving her one-time lover around, and pretending he was nothing more than her boss when he'd taken ownership of her heart, invaded her dreams and occupied most of her thoughts was going to be a huge ask.

Lex felt the burn of tears in her eyes, pulled her sunglasses off the top of her head and dropped them over her eyes. She couldn't let him see her cry...

Lex sniffed, took a deep breath and told herself, yet again, that she'd be okay, that she wouldn't feel heartbroken for ever. That, hopefully some time soon, she'd feel less sad, less...

Empty.

She was as busy as she'd ever been. The girls were back from their holiday, had started a new term at school and she was preparing for upcoming exams. She'd taken on a new student whose French was abysmal but who was prepared to pay her double her normal tutoring rate and she'd done the occasional delivery and pick-up for Thorpe Industries. But Lex felt like a spectator in her own life, as if she was standing outside of herself and watching herself run around. She was present but also not.

Because, honestly, seventy percent of her brain and all of her heart and soul was focused on Cole— wondering where he was, what he was doing, if he even missed her a fraction of the amount she missed him. Her world was in grayscale, her emotions muted, and she doubted whether she'd ever feel whole again.

She really hoped she would. But when? In two weeks? Two years? Twenty?

Lex saw the doorman step up to the door, her heart rate accelerated and all the moisture disappeared in her mouth. *Right, well, here goes nothing...*

She pulled out of her spot, cursing when the car jerked, and pulled up in front of the entrance, her eyes on Cole as he exchanged words with the doorman.

He wore light-grey trousers and a dark-navy jacket over a white shirt, and she immediately noticed he'd had his hair cut. She couldn't see his eyes because he wore dark sunglasses, but his face looked pale, and the smile he flashed at the doorman held none of its normal power.

He looked wonderful but tense. Was he as nervous at seeing her as she was seeing him? No, that wasn't possible. Cole did billion-dollar trades and invested ridiculous amounts of money in little-known products and business concepts. He was completely confident all the time and didn't tolerate nerves…

He walked over to the SUV and wrenched open the back passenger door. Lex closed her eyes when the scent of his cologne filled the car, remembering how she'd loved to bury her nose in his neck, in that soft place just below his jaw.

Be professional, Lex.

'Thank you for picking me up, Lex,' Cole said, after their eyes met in the rear-view mirror.

'Sure' She shrugged. 'It's my job.'

'How have you been?' he asked, and Lex wondered if she imagined the crack in his voice or whether she was projecting her jumpiness onto him.

'Fine. You?'

'Fine.'

Lex was quite certain that, within the space of thirty seconds, both their noses had grown two inches. She could see rigidity in his jaw and the tension in his shoulders. Her expression was no doubt grim. They were anything but *fine*.

She didn't bother to contain her sigh. 'Where am I taking you, Cole?'

He reached across and handed her a slip of paper, and Lex plugged the address into the on-board GPS.

He wanted her to drive him to Upper Constantia, to a very luxurious area called The Avenues, populated by mansions sitting on huge plots of land.

She started to ask him why he was going to a private address and then remembered that she had no right to pry into his business.

His choice, not hers.

Lex stopped at ten-feet-high wrought-iron gates and Cole leaned between the seats to aim the remote at the control box. As instructed, he pushed the blue button and the gates swung open. 'Follow the driveway and park in front of the house,' he told Lex and grimaced at his croaky voice.

He felt fifteen again, weak-kneed in the presence of his biggest crush. He rubbed his jaw, smoothed back his hair and looked out of the window, automatically clocking the massive oak trees, the huge swathe of lawn and the pretty single-storey, historic Victorian homestead.

Nice. He liked it.

He'd traded tens of billions of dollars, and made some ballsy choices business-wise, but this was his biggest ever gamble to date. For the first time, he felt queasy. He wasn't only gambling with a couple of million pounds—petty change—but with his heart, his future.

What if he'd missed his chance, screwed this all up by letting her down, by not taking her to Europe, for not allowing her to go with him to Thailand? What if he'd missed the boat?

What if…?

His rollicking thoughts were interrupted by Lex stopping the car. Thinking he'd jump out of his skin if he didn't move, he exited the car and walked towards the front door of the house. He was halfway there when he realised that Lex wasn't following.

He stopped, closed his eyes and shook his head. Turning, he walked back to the SUV and jerked open her door. Needing to see her eyes, he gently pulled off her sunglasses and placed them on the dashboard. He stared at her, taking in her glossy curls and her sexy mouth, and didn't miss the trepidation in her deep green eyes. Nobody, least of all him, should make her feel anxious or nervous. He looked into her lovely eyes, still full of hurt, and cursed himself for being a fool.

Walking away from her had been the dumbest move he'd ever made. She was what he needed and, if he wanted her in his life, he was going to have to fight for her. Fight his urges to run, to bail, to protect himself. He'd take anything she would give him, any time she could spare from her busy life looking after her sisters and pursuing her degree.

He was done living alone, being alone. And Lex was the only woman he could imagine being in his life full-time, for ever. Thinking that they couldn't have any barriers between them, he yanked off his sunglasses and tucked them into the inside pocket of his jacket. He held out his hand to Lex.

She looked from his hand to his eyes and back to his hand. 'Why are we here, Cole?'

'I have some things to say. Will you listen?'

She ignored his hand, hopped down from the car and jammed her hands into the back pockets of her pale-blue jeans. She shrugged and looked around. 'Where are we?'

'This property dates back to the late-eighteenth century. It's around five thousand square metres and is one of the biggest in the area. Five bedrooms, a three-bedroom cottage, staff accommodation and an apartment over the four-car garage.' He pointed up and Lex followed his gaze and shrugged.

'So?' When he didn't answer, she threw her hands up in the air. 'Cole, why are you acting like an estate agent? Why am I here?'

He didn't want to have this conversation standing on the driveway, so he took her hand and pulled her around the empty house and onto the entertainment deck overlooking one of the two pools on the property. The house was currently unoccupied, and he'd purchased it fully furnished, so he guided Lex over to a comfortable couch under the veranda roof.

If she agreed to his crazy plan, exploring the house could come later...

Right now, he had a *lot* of explaining to do.

Lex sat down on the couch and Cole pushed back the sturdy wooden coffee-table to make room for their legs. He sat down on the coffee table and rested his forearms on his thighs, inching to touch her.

But that, hopefully, would come later too.

Just say the words. Just get it done, Thorpe.

'I need to tell you who Charlie is.'

Surprise flashed in her eyes and a tiny frown pulled her eyebrows together. It was obvious that wasn't what she'd expected him to say. 'Okay…' She drawled out the word.

'The reason I cancelled our French jaunt was because Sam, my brother, asked for a meeting in Thailand,' Cole explained. 'He wanted to tell me about Charlie.'

'He couldn't email you the information?' Lex asked, sceptical.

'No, and I now understand why.' He swallowed, looked down at his hands, and rubbed the back of his neck. It was still so hard to comprehend, hard to take in.

'Charlie was my sister, Lex.'

He rubbed his hand over his jaw, still having difficulty with the words. 'She was ten months younger than me, and was apparently the centre of our family. A beautiful little girl and utterly adored, especially by my dad.'

Lex wrinkled her nose, trying to make sense of his words. 'I don't understand how you never knew you had a sister.'

He hadn't either and it had taken much convincing from Sam for him to believe that he'd once been a big brother.

'She died when I was very young.'

He felt Lex's hand slide over his knee and he immediately felt calmer, more in control. He wasn't alone, he had someone supporting him. He knew he wanted her, but until this moment he hadn't known how much he *needed* her. Her strength and her calm, her support.

'Tell me what happened, Cole,' Lex said.

'Please know that it wasn't my fault. Sam said it was a freak accident and I was hurt as well,' he gabbled, surprised to know that he could talk so fast.

Lex placed her hands on his face and forced him to look at her. 'Cole, darling, take a breath and tell me, as simply as possible, what happened.'

Simple. Good idea. Right now, simple was all he could handle.

Cole hauled in a deep breath, nodding once before speaking again. 'The original owner of Rossdale and my father met somewhere and became friends and he invited our family to what was, as Sam explained, quite a rustic place. It was more of a family holiday home than an inn and, apparently, my father fell in love with the place and they visited as often as they could.'

'Go on,' Lex murmured.

'Before it was renovated, it had a steep stone staircase. I was nearly four, Charlie was ten months younger than me. My mum put me and Charlie in an upstairs bedroom for an afternoon nap, but I wanted to play in the snow. Charlie and I left the room. There was a gate at the top of the stairs to keep us from going down the stairs on our own but it wasn't bolted. Nobody knows how it happened, but Charlie fell down the stairs. Sam thinks I tried to grab her and tumbled down after her. She died on impact. I was in a coma for a few days with a brain bleed. I woke up with no memory of the accident. Or her.'

Cole felt as if he was talking about a stranger, about another man who'd had a sister who'd died when he'd been little. How could he not remember anything of this?

'Oh, Cole,' Lex murmured.

'My father blamed my mother for not bolting the gate, my mum said she did. He said I must've managed to open it, but Sam says I wasn't tall or strong enough to do that. But it didn't matter to Grenville— Charlie's death was my mother's fault for not bolting it and my fault for letting her fall. Or for not dying instead of her,' he added.

He heard Lex's sharp intake of breath. 'No, Cole.'

He couldn't stop now. He had to get all of it out. It was the only way to lance the festering wound and put it behind him. 'He was a stone-hard man, someone incapable of emotion, and the little he did have when Charlie died transferred to Sam. He demanded a divorce and my mother agreed to go quietly, provided he never blamed me for, or even told me about, Charlie's death. He agreed because he didn't want anything more to do with either of us.'

'When did he buy Rossdale?' Lex asked.

'About five years after Charlie died. Every three months he'd make an offer, upping it until the owners couldn't refuse the insane money he was offering. Every year or so, around the anniversary of her death, he'd disappear for weeks at a time. When Sam realised he was at Rossdale on his own, drinking himself into a stupor, he challenged him to do something with the place, something that would honour Charlie's life. That's when he threw himself into renovating the property.'

'So, he rejected his own living flesh and blood and blamed you for her death, but remained emotionally connected to Charlie by turning the accident site into a shrine?' Lex asked, sounding incredulous. 'That's…that's so *sad*, Cole. And so selfish and narcissistic. It was all about *him*…his loss and his pain. And it was so easy for him to love Charlie. It didn't require much effort.'

He jerked up his head. 'What do you mean?'

'She died at a delightful age when she was sweet and lovely. She hadn't learned to talk back, to have an opinion, to argue with him or do her own thing. In his head, she was perfect and would be perfect for ever. That's not love, that's a cop-out. It takes courage to accept people with all their faults and foibles and love them anyway. Your father was an emotional coward.'

Of course he was. Cole dropped his head, ashamed that he'd craved Grenville's love and approval. It had taken over thirty years for him to realise his father had been emotionally stunted, an awful person who'd blamed his young son for his younger sister's death.

Because of Grenville, Cole had pushed away people, spent too much time alone and had second-guessed himself every step along the way, and for what? Because he'd thought that if he couldn't have his father, he'd become his father?

He didn't know what had happened that day at

the ski-lodge—honestly, he didn't even remember Charlie—but what he knew for sure was that he didn't have it within him to hurt anyone and that her death had been a horrible, horrible, tragic accident.

His father could've grieved for his daughter, loved his wife harder and gathered his sons closer. But Grenville had chosen to distance himself, to perpetuate the pain. And, the longer he'd lived in his cold, acid-tinged shadow, the more like him Cole had become. Cold. Bitter. Lonely.

He was done.

No more. It was time to step into the light. To love and be loved.

Lex lifted her fingers to her mouth and closed her eyes. She said a quiet prayer in Charlie's name.

The little girl who Cole had never known.

Lex did not doubt that Cole's mother had thought she was doing him a favour when she'd hidden the truth from him, thinking that he couldn't handle knowing that his sister had died when he'd lived, and that his father blamed him for her death. But Lex knew children were a lot more resilient than adults gave them credit for and that honesty was always the best way to go. As Cole had grown up, his mum could've told him what had happened, assured him the accident wasn't his fault and explained that his father couldn't move on.

Cole could've got therapy and a clearer picture of why his father had refused to interact with him.

'I thought that if I couldn't have a relationship with

him, then I couldn't have a relationship with anyone,' Cole said, every word coated with pain. 'I've had relationships but I've always cut and run. Because that's what my mum did emotionally, and what Grenville did emotionally *and* physically.'

Lex leaned forward, placed her hands on his knees and rested her forehead on his. 'I'm so sorry, Cole. I'm so sorry about Charlie.' She looked up. 'And you remember nothing about her?'

Cole pulled back and ducked his head. He pulled his hair apart and she saw a long, vicious scar. 'They told me I fell down some stairs, that's all I know. I don't have any memories from before waking up in hospital.'

'I can't believe your brother never told you, especially after both your parents died.'

Cole shrugged. 'Ignoring stuff was what we did. My parents divorced and ignored each other. My sister died and nobody mentioned her again. My family is very good at disconnecting. My brother just walked away from his life, and me, to become a monk.'

And Cole had walked away from her. Yeah, she could believe that it was a family trait. Cole, looking thoroughly miserable, pushed his hand through his hair. '"Just walk away" should be written on our family crest.'

Probably. And wasn't it her luck to fall in love with someone who did exactly what she'd experienced all her life? Could she pick them or what?

She now knew why he acted like he did, why he found it difficult to stick—he'd never been shown how to. But, as sad as his story was, however much she grieved for him, he'd walked away from her once and she wouldn't allow him to do that again. She couldn't take the chance of having her heart stomped on again.

It was her turn to go.

She stood up and raised her shoulders. 'I'm going to go. I need to collect Nixi and Snow from school.'

That wasn't for a couple of hours, but she couldn't stay here and be tortured by what she couldn't have. Seeing him was like backsliding into addiction again—one hit and she was toast. She'd be suffering withdrawal symptoms for days, possibly weeks, now.

'Don't go,' Cole said, his voice breaking.

What was the point of her staying? She was just prolonging the agony. 'Cole...'

'Please stay. Not just for now, but for ever. Please don't walk away from me.'

From a place far away, Lex heard the sound of the car keys hitting the floor and she jammed her hands into the back pockets of her jeans and told her feet to stay where they were. She was not going to run to him and throw himself in his arms.

Not just yet anyway.

'Why not?' she asked quietly. 'How are you going to persuade me to stay?'

If he said money and...stuff...she'd brain him with the rather lovely hand-blown glass bowl sitting on the coffee table behind him.

Cole walked towards her and stopped when they were just inches apart, close enough for her to go up onto her tiptoes and kiss the underside of his stubbled jaw. His hand cradled her face and Lex steeled herself not to react. Yes, her knees wanted to melt, yes, she wanted to kiss him and, yes, she wanted to stand in the protective band of his arms.

But if he couldn't give her what she most needed...

Cole's thumb brushed over her jaw. 'I'm not good at relationships, Lex, but I've been better with you in two weeks than I've ever been with anyone before. Something about you opened up something in me and, while I don't think I'll ever wear my heart on my sleeve as a matter of routine, I will with you. And with any children—yours, ours—that share our house and lives. I refuse to be like him—cold, selfish, alone, bitter. Unloved. Unable *to* love.'

Lex felt a ball in her chest and found she was struggling to take in enough air. She had no idea what to say, even where to start. Then Cole bracketed her face with his hands and he gently, so tenderly, swiped his mouth across hers.

'I love you, Lex, and I want to keep loving you for the rest of my life.'

She closed her eyes, thrilled to her core, infused with a blinding white light of pure joy. But there was still a whisper of doubt...

'Cole, you're saying everything I wanted to hear but—'

'But you are raising your sisters...you have Addi to think of...you have responsibilities,' he interrupted her. 'You also have a degree to finish and a career to start. Fine.'

She held his wrists and raised her eyebrows. 'What

does "fine" mean? How can I do that, and have a relationship with you when you live ten thousand miles away?'

He moved his hands to her hips and she noticed that his eyes had warmed to amber. 'I'm going to relocate and won't travel so much. I'll help with the school runs, I'll help with homework, I'm pretty good at maths…'

She held up her hand, a little overwhelmed. 'Wait, whoa. Are you suggesting that you move in with us?' Their house was tiny and there wasn't room for someone as big and bold as Cole.

'I was thinking that maybe you could move in with me. There's a massive house behind us that I've just bought, sweetheart.' He saw her shock and ignored it. 'If you say yes, then Addi could move into the guest house, your other sister can use the apartment over the garage and the younger girls can live with us and run between their and our houses. We can hire an au pair to look after the girls to free up some of your time so you can get your degree done. Bottom line, I just want to wake up every day in our bed with you in my arms, be in your life.'

Oh, man, that sounded like every dream she'd ever had coming thundering towards her but she still wasn't sure that he knew how much he was taking on. 'Cole, the girls are strong-willed and demanding. They are messy and loud. They fight and cry and are overly dramatic. They will be a constant part of my life for the next ten to twelve years.'

He placed a kiss on her cheek, then on her jaw, and

Lex found it hard to think. 'Of course they will. I understand that, in marrying you, I acquire four sisters, two of whom will be moving in with us. I get it, Lex, and I don't care. I would take on a whole orphanage of kids if that's what you wanted.'

Then he shrugged and Lex saw a hint of excitement in his eyes, a smidgeon of terror. 'I didn't have much to do with my brother, and don't remember my sister, so maybe I can share yours.'

He'd never had a family and she could see he was desperate for one. He needed the girly hugs and the drama, to come home to a house filled with love, noise, music and laughter. He needed a family more than he knew. But it still wasn't enough to dispel all her doubt that they could work.

'I'm terrified that in six months, a year, you'll decide that this, us, is too much and that you've made a mistake and you'll walk away,' Lex said, feeling a tiny crack form in her heart. 'I'm scared to take that risk, Cole, but I'm terrified for the girls. I won't have them hurt because you promised to love them and then walked away. I'd risk my heart, but not theirs.'

Cole held her eyes. 'I wish I could stand here and tell you that I'm going to be great at this immediately, Lex. But the truth is that I'll probably be overwhelmed and want to tear my hair out occasionally. But I promise you—I *promise* you—that I won't walk. I won't just wake up one morning and bail. I will stick and I will stay and we *will* work through everything life throws at us. It will be worth it. That I know,' he told her with complete conviction in his voice.

'How? How can you know that?' Lex demanded.

'Because we are better, stronger, happier together than we are apart, sweetheart.'

He was right. She could live a life without him, but it wouldn't be as much fun. Her heart wouldn't be as light and bright as it would be if he was around.

Cole cuddled her closer and rested his temple against hers. 'I've been looking for love my whole life, Lex. And your love is all I need.'

Lex encircled her arms around his waist and reached up to place her face in his neck, feeling every inch of her settling, sighing, relaxing. Cole was holding her and all was right with her world.

'I love you,' she whispered quietly.

'I love you more, my darling.' He pulled back and pushed her hair off her forehead, tucking a curl behind her ear. Their eyes connected and she saw his throat bob. 'Be mine?'

Every inch of her smiled. 'I have been. I am. I always will be.'

Cole covered her mouth with his, banded his arm around her hips and lifted her up and into him. Lex wrapped her legs around his hips and placed kisses on his cheek and jaw, the side of his nose. 'I think we should call our first child Charlie,' she said.

Cole's smile was sweeter than she'd ever seen it. 'I think that's a very good idea. Shall we start working on that right now?'

Lex laughed. 'I'm brave, but not that brave, Cole.

Let's put a baby on hold for a year or two, or three or four.'

He sent her a wicked grin as he walked her into the house, heading for the nearest couch, she presumed. 'You let me know when, sweetheart. I'm always up for the challenge.'

He was. And always would be.

* * * * *

Caught up in the intensity of
The Nights She Spent with the CEO?
Make sure to look out for the next instalment of the
Cape Town Tycoons duet,
coming soon!

In the meantime, get your next romance fix
with these other stories by Joss Wood!

How to Tempt the Off-Limits Billionaire
The Rules of Their Red-Hot Reunion
The Billionaire's One-Night Baby
The Powerful Boss She Craves
The Twin Secret She Must Reveal

Available now!

COMING NEXT MONTH FROM

H HARLEQUIN
PRESENTS

#4089 THE BABY THE DESERT KING MUST CLAIM
by Lynne Graham

When chef Claire is introduced to her elusive employer, she gets the shock of her life! Because the royal that Claire has been working for is Raif, father to the baby Claire's *just* discovered she's carrying!

#4090 A SECRET HEIR TO SECURE HIS THRONE
by Caitlin Crews

Grief-stricken Paris Apollo is intent on getting revenge for his parents' deaths. And he's just discovered a shocking secret: his son! A legitimate heir will mean a triumphant return to power—*if* Madelyn will marry him...

#4091 BOUND BY THE ITALIAN'S "I DO"
A Billion-Dollar Revenge
by Michelle Smart

Billionaire Gianni destroyed Issy's family legacy. Now, it's time for payback by taking down his company! Then Gianni calls her bluff with an outrageous marriage proposal. And Issy must make one last move...by saying *yes*!

#4092 HIS INNOCENT FOR ONE SPANISH NIGHT
Heirs to the Romero Empire
by Carol Marinelli

Alej's desire for photographer Emily is held at bay solely by his belief she's too innocent for someone so cynical. Until one passionate encounter becomes irresistible! The trouble is, now Alej knows exactly how electric they are together...

HPCNMRA0223

#4093 THE GREEK'S FORGOTTEN MARRIAGE
by Maya Blake

Imogen has finally tracked down her missing husband, Zeph. But he has no recollection of their business-deal union! Yet as Zeph slowly pieces his memories together, one thing is for certain: this time, an on-paper marriage won't be enough!

#4094 RETURNING FOR HIS RUTHLESS REVENGE
by Louise Fuller

When self-made Gabriel hires attorney Dove, it's purely business—unfinished business, that is. Years ago, she broke his heart...now he'll force her to face him! Yet their chemistry is undeniable. Will they finally finish what they started?

#4095 RECLAIMED BY HIS BILLION-DOLLAR RING
by Julia James

It's been eight years since Nikos left Calanthe without a goodbye. Now, becoming the Greek's bride is the only way to help her ailing father. Even if it feels like she's walking back into the lion's den...

#4096 ENGAGED TO LONDON'S WILDEST BILLIONAIRE
Behind the Palace Doors...
by Kali Anthony

Lance's debauched reputation is the stuff of tabloid legend. But entertaining thoughts of his attraction to sheltered Sara would be far too reckless. Then she makes him an impassioned plea to help her escape an arranged wedding. His solution? Their own headline-making engagement!

YOU CAN FIND MORE INFORMATION ON UPCOMING HARLEQUIN TITLES, FREE EXCERPTS AND MORE AT HARLEQUIN.COM.

HPCNMRB0223

Get 4 FREE REWARDS!

We'll send you 2 FREE Books plus 2 FREE Mystery Gifts.

FREE Value Over **$20**

Both the **Harlequin® Desire** and **Harlequin Presents®** series feature compelling novels filled with passion, sensuality and intriguing scandals.

YES! Please send me 2 FREE novels from the Harlequin Desire or Harlequin Presents series and my 2 FREE gifts (gifts are worth about $10 retail). After receiving them, if I don't wish to receive any more books, I can return the shipping statement marked "cancel." If I don't cancel, I will receive 6 brand-new Harlequin Presents Larger-Print books every month and be billed just $6.30 each in the U.S. or $6.49 each in Canada, a savings of at least 10% off the cover price, or 6 Harlequin Desire books every month and be billed just $5.05 each in the U.S. or $5.74 each in Canada, a savings of at least 12% off the cover price. It's quite a bargain! Shipping and handling is just 50¢ per book in the U.S. and $1.25 per book in Canada.* I understand that accepting the 2 free books and gifts places me under no obligation to buy anything. I can always return a shipment and cancel at any time by calling the number below. The free books and gifts are mine to keep no matter what I decide.

Choose one: ☐ **Harlequin Desire**
(225/326 HDN GRJ7)

☐ **Harlequin Presents Larger-Print**
(176/376 HDN GRJ7)

Name (please print)

Address   Apt. #

City   State/Province   Zip/Postal Code

Email: Please check this box ☐ if you would like to receive newsletters and promotional emails from Harlequin Enterprises ULC and its affiliates. You can unsubscribe anytime.

Mail to the **Harlequin Reader Service:**
IN U.S.A.: P.O. Box 1341, Buffalo, NY 14240-8531
IN CANADA: P.O. Box 603, Fort Erie, Ontario L2A 5X3

Want to try 2 free books from another series? Call 1-800-873-8635 or visit www.ReaderService.com.

*Terms and prices subject to change without notice. Prices do not include sales taxes, which will be charged (if applicable) based on your state or country of residence. Canadian residents will be charged applicable taxes. Offer not valid in Quebec. This offer is limited to one order per household. Books received may not be as shown. Not valid for current subscribers to the Harlequin Presents or Harlequin Desire series. All orders subject to approval. Credit or debit balances in a customer's account(s) may be offset by any other outstanding balance owed by or to the customer. Please allow 4 to 6 weeks for delivery. Offer available while quantities last.

Your Privacy—Your information is being collected by Harlequin Enterprises ULC, operating as Harlequin Reader Service. For a complete summary of the information we collect, how we use this information and to whom it is disclosed, please visit our privacy notice located at corporate.harlequin.com/privacy-notice. From time to time we may also exchange your personal information with reputable third parties. If you wish to opt out of this sharing of your personal information, please visit readerservice.com/consumerschoice or call 1-800-873-8635. **Notice to California Residents**—Under California law, you have specific rights to control and access your data. For more information on these rights and how to exercise them, visit corporate.harlequin.com/california-privacy.

HDHP22R3

HARLEQUIN
PLUS

Try the best multimedia subscription service for romance readers like you!

Read, Watch and Play.

Experience the easiest way to get the romance content you crave.

Start your **FREE TRIAL** at
www.harlequinplus.com/freetrial.

HARPLUS0123